TOO GOOD TO BE TRUE

Tori listened quietly as her friends went on about Elyse Taylor. It was hard not to be jealous of the famous skater. Elyse had everything Tori wanted—a gold medal, great looks, and the admiration of millions.

"Elyse is perfect," Nikki said. "I hope I'll be exactly like that when I get to the Nationals—and the Olympics."

"Not me," Haley said. "I mean, give me a break. Elyse *is* perfect. Too perfect. It almost makes me want to gag—you know what I mean?"

"No way!" Nikki cried.

"You've got to be kidding," Danielle said.

"I'm not," Haley said. "I mean, she's too nice. Don't you think it's an act? How can one person be so nice all the time?"

THE ICE PRINCESS

Melissa Lowell

Created by Parachute Press

A SKYLARK BOOK
NEW YORK · TORONTO · LONDON · SYDNEY · AUCKLAND

RL 5.0, 009-012

THE ICE PRINCESS
A Skylark Book / January 1995

Skylark Books is a registered trademark of Bantam Books, a division
of Bantam Doubleday Dell Publishing Group, Inc. Registered in U.S.
Patent and Trademark Office and elsewhere.

Series design: Barbara Berger

ISBN 0-553-48289-0

Published simultaneously in the United States and Canada

Bantam Books are published by Bantam Books, a division of Bantam Doubleday
Dell Publishing Group, Inc. Its trademark, consisting of the words "Bantam
Books" and the portrayal of a rooster, is Registered in U.S. Patent and Trademark
Office and in other countries. Marca Registrada. Bantam Books, 1540 Broadway,
New York, New York 10036.

PRINTED IN THE UNITED STATES OF AMERICA

OPM 0 9 8 7 6 5 4 3 2

1

"**T**urn up the TV! I want to hear what she's saying!" Tori Carsen urged. She reached out from her spot on the sofa and gave her friend Haley Arthur a quick poke with her toes.

It was Sunday afternoon, and Tori and her friends were hanging out in Tori's family room. Sprawled on the rug next to Haley were Nikki Simon and Danielle Panati. All four girls were members of Silver Blades, one of the best figure-skating clubs in the country. On most afternoons they would be on the ice practicing, but today was Sunday, their day off. They were just relaxing, waiting to see Elyse Taylor, the recent Olympic gold-medal winner, appear on TV.

Haley grabbed the remote control from the floor

and clicked the volume button. Almost instantly the television in the family room boomed.

"I'll never forget it," Elyse Taylor said on TV. "It was like watching a movie of someone else's life. I've been dreaming about winning an Olympic gold medal ever since I was four years old, but when it finally happened, I felt like I wasn't really there."

"Oh, you were there, all right," the TV interviewer joked with the beautiful nineteen-year-old skater. "Hundreds of millions of people saw you skate that magnificent program."

"I know," Elyse Taylor said, giggling. "That's why today is so special to me. Coming home to New Hampshire and having this parade in my hometown—*now* I really feel like an Olympic champion."

The television camera pulled back to reveal Elyse Taylor and the interviewer standing on a crowded street in a small town. Behind them marching bands and decorated floats were lined up for the parade that was about to take place. Crowds of people pressed in, trying to see the famous figure skater. Elyse wore a sequined royal-blue chiffon skating dress—the one she had worn to win the Olympic gold medal just a few weeks before.

Nikki grabbed a pillow and scooted in closer to the TV. "I wish I looked like Elyse," she said, smoothing her brown hair and self-consciously covering up her braces with her hand. "She's so lucky," Nikki went on. "Everything about her is perfect. Her hair. Her smile. Her skating. Especially her personality. She's so nice!"

"I know," Danielle agreed. "And I've read that she never has to worry about her weight either. She can eat anything!" Danielle, who had honey-brown hair and dark-brown eyes and was slightly plump, was always watching what she ate.

"Her jumps are incredible," Haley added.

"And look at that outfit," Nikki moaned. "It's totally beautiful! It's just as beautiful as your skating dresses, Tori. And *that's* saying something!"

Tori smiled. She knew her friends were envious of her skating clothes. But what could she do? Her mother was a successful fashion designer and often designed dresses for Tori. Mrs. Carsen had taught Tori that it was important to dress beautifully, even for practice, so that she'd always feel like a great performer and star.

"That dress cost thirteen *thousand* dollars," Haley remarked. "I heard that a famous designer in New York City made it."

"I know," Danielle said. "Do you believe she's going to wear that skating dress in the parade? In *March*? It's freezing outside."

"She's probably just doing it for her fans," Nikki replied. "So everyone can take pictures of her and see the dress again. I've read that she never turns down requests for autographs."

"I know," Danielle said for the third time.

"Dani—if you don't stop saying 'I know'—you're going to drive me crazy!" Haley complained.

"I know," Danielle said, and everyone laughed.

Tori listened quietly as her friends went on about Elyse Taylor. It was hard not to be jealous of the famous skater. Elyse had everything Tori wanted—a gold medal, great looks, and the admiration of millions. She was also one of the most popular skaters in the world. Whenever Elyse talked about competition, she always emphasized giving her all—not beating other skaters. And she was always gracious when she didn't come in first, never complaining about the judging or the other skaters, at least not publicly. There didn't seem to be a mean bone in Elyse's body.

Secretly Tori wished she could be more like Elyse—a strong competitor who wasn't out to totally *crush* the competition. For Tori the desire to win—and please her pushy mother—was often stronger than anything else. More than once she had even let her competitiveness get in the way of her friendships. She blushed, thinking about how she'd lied to Nikki shortly after Nikki had joined Silver Blades, saying that Nikki's coach thought Nikki was a lousy skater. The truth was Nikki was a fabulous skater, and Tori had been desperate to get her to quit the club. Now Tori was sorry about what she'd done, and she and Nikki were close friends.

"Elyse is perfect," Nikki said again. "I hope I'll

be exactly like that when I get to the Nationals—
and the Olympics."

Me too, Tori thought, brushing a blond curl out
of her blue eyes.

"Not me," Haley said, suddenly sitting up and
turning around to look at her friends. Haley's red
hair was sticking straight up on one side, where
she had been lying on it. But as usual Haley didn't
seem to care at all about keeping her hair neat. She
was a year younger than the other three skaters but
she acted older than twelve. And one of the reasons
Tori liked her was she had her own distinctive style.
Today she was in baggy jeans, combat boots, heavy
neon-colored socks, and a small silver-dagger earring in one ear.

"I mean, give me a break," Haley went on. "Elyse
is perfect. Too perfect. It almost makes me want to
gag—you know what I mean?"

"No way!" Nikki cried.

"You've got to be kidding," Danielle said.

"I'm not," Haley said. "I mean, she's *too* nice.
Don't you think it's an act? How can any one person
be so nice all the time?"

"That's what makes her so great," Danielle explained. "She never acts petty, the way a lot of
skaters do."

"Yeah, maybe." Haley shrugged. "But I think it's
sort of weird. No one's that nice all the time," she
insisted.

"Shhh!" Tori said, waving her hand up and down.
"She's on again. I'm trying to listen."

Instantly Nikki, Danielle, and Haley stopped talking and turned back to the TV. Elyse was in the middle of a sentence.

". . . thank everyone and let them know that I just want to give something back to all the people who helped me over the years," Elyse said.

"Is that why you've decided to do a benefit performance for a children's hospital in Pennsylvania next week?" the interviewer asked.

Elyse nodded. "It's the least I can do," she said with a small, humble shrug. Then the interviewer thanked her and cut away to a commercial.

"Pennsylvania?" Danielle screamed. "She's coming here? When? Where? We've got to find out so we can get tickets and go!"

"That would be so cool!" Nikki said. "Maybe we can get my mother to drive us. I mean, depending on where it is."

"Yeah, but this is a big state," Haley reminded them. "I mean, what if she's coming to someplace three hundred miles away?"

"It doesn't matter," Tori said, speaking up for the first time. "We'll all go together. I'm sure my mother will get us tickets, no matter where it is."

Suddenly Danielle gasped. "Hey, guys," she cried, jumping up and looking at her watch. "I just remembered. There's a meeting at the rink today—with Blake Michaels to talk about the new ice show!"

"You're right," Tori said, scrambling to her feet. "I can't believe we forgot about it. Let's go!"

As everyone in Silver Blades knew, Blake Michaels was the youngest, best-looking, and most graceful ice dancer to hit the skating scene in years. He had recently placed third in the World competition, and he probably would have won a medal in the Olympics if his partner hadn't been seriously injured in a terrible fall during practice. Blake had retired from amateur skating, and now at the age of twenty-three he was making a career as a skating choreographer. He had arrived in Seneca Hills just last week, and Tori already had a crush on him. A major crush. After spending days trying to impress him, she hoped she hadn't blown it by forgetting about today's meeting. She'd never forgive herself.

Twenty minutes later Tori's mom pulled up in front of Seneca Hills Ice Arena.

"How long will you be?" Mrs. Carson called to Tori as the four girls jumped out of the car. "Are you going to practice today?"

"No way," Tori answered, looking at the number of cars in the parking lot. "It's too crowded. You can pick us up in an hour."

Seneca Hills Ice Arena was really two skating rinks, side by side, under one roof. One was used for figure skating. The other was used for hockey practices and games. Tori could tell from the parking lot that both rinks were crowded with kids, parents, teenagers, and couples who had come to skate just for the fun of it. Sunday afternoon was an open session on the figure-skating rink, and none of the Silver Blades skaters liked to skate then. The ice was too packed with people racing around in circles or struggling to stand up. Serious skaters couldn't practice their jumps on such a crowded surface.

As Tori hurried to get out of the cold winter air, she pulled her bright blue parka tightly around her and rushed past her three friends and through the front doors. She was going so fast, she didn't notice the man coming out and almost ran smack into him. When she looked up, she saw it was Blake Michaels. He wore a tight black sweater with faded pale blue jeans and a pale blue parka—an outfit that perfectly matched his jet-black hair and pale blue eyes.

"Hey!" he said, slowing his stride and flashing a big smile at Tori and her friends. "What happened to you guys? I thought you weren't going to show."

"We forgot all about the meeting," Danielle said apologetically. "Is it over?"

"Yeah," Blake said, "but you didn't miss much. I called all the skaters together because I thought we were going to start planning a big ice show for the spring—and I wanted to talk about the choreography. But the Silver Blades board of directors wants to hold off the show for a while. So I'm going to work with you individually instead."

Tori held her breath. *Please* say you're going to choreograph a program for me.

Tori knew that working with a choreographer like Blake could make a big difference in her skating career. The choreographer was the one who arranged a skater's jumps and spins and set the whole routine to music. A beautifully choreographed program would make Tori's skating style and ability even more impressive—and would win points with judges for sure. There was a Regional competition coming up in a few months—Tori would love to have a new program ready for that.

"I'm going to choreograph a program for several skaters in Silver Blades," Blake continued. "And after talking to your coaches, I've decided to start with the two people who need me the most—Haley Arthur and Patrick McGuire."

"Yes!" Haley said, sticking a triumphant fist in the air.

Haley and Patrick had come together as a pairs skating team just a few months ago, right after Haley's old partner moved to Japan. Their coach, Kathy Bart, had been saying they needed a new program, something of their own, and now it looked as if they'd be getting it.

Tori knew Blake's decision was fair, but she could still feel a knot forming in her stomach. How could Blake pick Haley and Patrick first? Didn't he know that Tori wanted to work with him more than anyone else in Silver Blades? Or that she was one of the most talented skaters in the club?

"That's great," Nikki congratulated Haley. "You and Patrick deserve it."

"Yeah, way to go, Haley," Danielle added.

"How long do you think it will take?" Tori asked Blake, looking up into his sparkling blue eyes.

Blake laughed. "That depends on Haley and Patrick," he said. "But I'd say I should be finished with them in a couple of weeks."

"And then who's next?" Tori asked quickly.

"I'm not sure," Blake said.

Tori glanced quickly at Nikki and Danielle, who were exchanging looks. They want to be next, too, Tori realized. She had to find away to get Blake to pick her. This was a great opportunity, and she couldn't afford to miss it.

"There was one more exciting piece of news that you missed," Blake added, a teasing twinkle in his eye.

"What?" Nikki asked.

"An old friend of mine called me last night," he explained. "She's coming to Seneca Hills for a week, and I think you girls might like to meet her."

"Cool," Haley said. "Who is she?"

"Actually I think it's someone you might have heard of." The smile spread broadly across Blake's face. "She's a skater. An Olympic skater. Her name is Elyse Taylor."

2

"Elyse Taylor? Coming here?" Tori almost yelled the words. A few people in the lobby of the ice rink looked over at her and stared.

Blake laughed again. "I thought you'd be interested," he said with a wide grin.

"Interested? You've got to be kidding!" Nikki cried. "This is totally cool!"

"We just saw Elyse on TV," Danielle added. "She mentioned she was coming to Pennsylvania—but she didn't say it was Seneca Hills!"

"She didn't?" Blake asked. "I'll have to yell at her for that. Our skating club could use the publicity, and she knows it."

"But how do you know her?" Tori asked.

"We're . . . old friends," Blake answered quickly. "Anyway she had a sudden cancellation in her touring schedule, so she called and offered to come here for a week as a guest coach. She'll do skating clinics and teach a few private lessons, and next Sunday night she'll give a performance to benefit the children's hospital."

"I can't believe it," Nikki said. "We're going to meet Elyse Taylor—tomorrow!"

"But will we really get to take lessons from her?" Danielle asked uncertainly.

"Yes!" Blake laughed at the look of disbelief on her face.

Tori's mind drifted for a moment as she thought about what it would be like to meet the famous skater. Would Elyse see right away that Tori was one of the most talented skaters in Silver Blades? Maybe she can give me some inside information on how to win over judges at competitions, she thought. Or even talk Blake into choreographing his next program for me. Elyse's visit might turn out to be the best thing that ever happened to Tori's career!

"I've got to go," Blake said. "I'm going to see if I can book a room for Elyse at one of the hotels in town."

"She can stay at my house," Tori suddenly blurted out while Nikki, Danielle, and Haley were still talking.

Everyone stared at her.

"Really?" Blake asked. He thought for a minute, then nodded. "That would be great. I know Elyse gets sick of staying in hotels all the time. She'd probably love to stay in someone's home. But are you sure you don't need to check with your mother first?"

"Not at all," Tori said, tossing her long blond hair over her shoulders. She couldn't help letting a smug smile show on her face. "My mother will love having Elyse stay with us."

Inside, Tori hoped this was true. Her mother wasn't usually crazy about having houseguests. But for someone as famous as Elyse Taylor, Mrs. Carsen might make an exception. Especially when she could help Tori's career.

"That will be cool," Haley said, sounding only a little jealous. "Maybe we can all come over to your house and have dinner with her."

"Uh, sure," Tori agreed reluctantly. "I mean, if she has time. But we have to give her some privacy while she's here, you know. She might not want a whole bunch of people constantly hanging around her."

"Right, Tori," Danielle remarked with a knowing glance. Obviously she knew Tori was hoping to keep Elyse to herself. Tori felt her face flush.

"Well, I'll see you," Blake called, heading toward the door. "But thanks, Tori, for offering to have Elyse as a guest. That takes a lot of pressure off me."

What does that mean? Tori wondered. Didn't Blake want to spend time with Elyse?

"I'm picking her up at the airport tomorrow at two," Blake went on as he pushed open the glass front door. "I'll drop her off at your house after that." Then he let the door swing closed as he walked to his car.

"He's really nice," Haley said. "No wonder he and Elyse are friends."

"I still can't believe she's coming to Seneca Hills," Nikki said. "Wait until Jill hears about this."

"For once *she'll* be jealous of *us*!" Danielle said with a little laugh.

Jill Wong had been one of the best skaters in Silver Blades, and she was another one of Tori's closest friends. But recently she had moved to Denver, Colorado, to attend the International Ice Academy. Since then Tori and her friends rarely saw her, but they kept in touch with Jill by writing letters and calling whenever there was news. Tori could hardly wait to tell Jill that she was going to have the newest Olympic champion staying at her house for a whole week!

"I need to talk to Kathy about my practice schedule," Nikki said, interrupting Tori's thoughts. "My mom has some doctor appointments and can't drive me here certain days. Anybody want to come?"

"Go visit the Sarge? On our one day off? No thanks," Danielle said.

"Kathy's not so bad," Nikki said. "I'm getting used to her." Tori smiled. She knew how everyone felt about Kathy Bart, one of the two coaches for Silver Blades. Kathy, who was in her late twenties, was known for being so tough on her students that everyone called her "Sarge" behind her back. Tori's coach for over five years was Franz Weiler, an older man who had won a silver medal in the Olympics many years ago. Tori didn't always get along with Kathy, but she respected her as a great skater. And since Tori trained with Mr. Weiler, not Kathy, she wasn't quite as nervous around Kathy as some of the other skaters were.

"I'll come with you," Tori offered.

"I'm going to check out the action on the hockey rink," Haley announced. Haley had a lot of guys as friends, so she often hung out with the hockey team. "Come on, Danielle."

Tori and Nikki walked down the hall to Kathy's office as their friends went the other way. On the way Tori asked Nikki about her mother. Tori thought it was so cool that Mrs. Simon was pregnant. In several months Nikki would have a baby brother or sister, while Tori would still be the only child in her house. She often thought having a brother or sister would help relieve some of the pressure her mother put on her.

Kathy was on the phone, but she motioned the girls to come in. After she hung up, Nikki explained the problem, and the two of them bent over a scheduling book to work out times for Nikki's private sessions.

While they talked, Tori gazed at the books, trophies, and awards that filled Kathy's shelves and the framed photos that hung on her walls. There was a picture of Kathy wearing a green satin skating dress trimmed in gold braid.

It looks totally out of date, Tori thought, smiling. Tori knew it was one of the outfits Kathy had worn when she was still competing. Kathy had placed fourth in the Nationals, the highest-level competition in the United States. If she had placed in the top three, she would have gone on to the Worlds or the Olympics that year.

"Hey—you have an autographed picture of Margo DeForest," Tori said, staring at a black-and-white photo on Kathy's wall.

Margo DeForest had been a champion skater many years before. In fact, she was one of the first American gold medalists. Tori wasn't sure why, but older figure skaters always talked about Margo as if she were some kind of major legend.

Kathy looked up and smiled. "She was my idol when I was a little girl."

Tori glanced back at the photo. Now that she looked more carefully, something about the look on Margo's face reminded Tori of Kathy. They both wore the confident, determined expression of champions.

Tori also noticed that in the picture, Margo wore her hair in a loose, low ponytail tied with a big bow—exactly the same way Kathy wore her own long dark-blond hair.

Then Tori saw a faded, red hardcover book on the top shelf in Kathy's office. "You have a copy of her autobiography, too?" Tori asked.

Kathy nodded.

"Can I borrow it?" Tori asked, taking the book off the shelf. Something about the skater intrigued her.

"No," Kathy said with a firm shake of her head. "I never lend my books, and especially not that one. It's very old and very valuable. But you're welcome to look at it here in my office."

Tori sat down and opened the book. On the cover it said *My Story* by Margo DeForest.

Inside the cover, in dark-blue fountain-pen ink, there was a message written. It said, "To Kathy Bart, A fine young skater with the heart of a champion. Best of luck always, Margo DeForest."

Wow, Tori thought, an autographed copy. Kathy must have met Margo DeForest during her career.

Settling into the saggy canvas director's chair in the corner of Kathy's office, Tori started to read the book from page one. It was an amazing story about Margo's lonely childhood after her brother died, her struggle to overcome rheumatic fever, and her determination to become a top figure skater, no matter how much hard work and sacrifice it took.

"Tori?"

Tori looked up. Nikki stood there staring at her. Kathy had left the room.

"I'm done here. Time to go."

"Oh," Tori said, glancing at the book in her hands. "I, uh, just want to read a little bit more. Can I meet you in the lobby?"

"Sure," Nikki said. "But your mom will be here to pick us up pretty soon, won't she?"

"I'll be right there," Tori promised, putting her head back in the book.

As she read on, Tori found herself getting more and more involved in Margo's story. It seemed as if she had had to work for everything. What moved Tori the most was the fact that Margo's parents didn't push her to be a skater. It was completely her own choice. Tori's mother, on the other hand, pushed Tori all the time. Mrs. Carsen was determined that her daughter become a champion. And even though that was what Tori wanted, too, sometimes it was hard to have such a demanding parent. Especially since it was just Tori and her mother. Her parents were divorced, and she rarely saw her father.

"Are you still here?" The voice startled Tori, and she jumped. It was Kathy.

"Sorry," Tori said, standing up and closing the book. "I just got so wrapped up in this story."

"Your mother is outside waiting for you," Kathy said.

Tori held the book tightly to her chest. "Can I come back and read some more tomorrow?" Tori asked.

Kathy cocked her head to one side and smiled. "It's a great story, isn't it?" she said. "Margo DeForest was not only a great skater, she was a true champion . . ." Kathy's voice trailed off as she studied Tori closely. "I'll tell you what," she said. "I'll let you borrow the book—but just for a few days. And you have to *promise* me that nothing will happen to it, Tori. That book is very special to me."

Tori's face lit up. "Thanks!" she said. "Don't worry. I'll take good care of it. I promise."

What a great day, Tori thought, racing down the hall to find her friends and meet her mother. Elyse Taylor was coming to Seneca Hills and would be staying at Tori's house. And she couldn't wait to finish reading Margo DeForest's autobiography.

The one thing that would make today perfect, Tori thought, was finding a way to get Blake Michaels's attention. But now that Elyse Taylor was coming to town, Tori had a good idea about how to do just that.

3

"Is she here yet?" Tori asked anxiously as she climbed into her mother's silver Jaguar after skating practice on Monday afternoon.

"Her plane was late," Mrs. Carsen answered. "Blake called and said she'd arrive within half an hour. They're probably on their way to our house now."

Out of the corner of her eye Tori watched her mother. Was she nervous or excited? It was hard to tell. Last night, when Tori told her that she had invited Elyse to stay with them, Mrs. Carsen had blown up. But once the idea of having an Olympic skating star as a guest sank in, Mrs. Carsen became as excited as Tori. She raced around straightening up the house, baking a special dessert, and grilling Tori nonstop about Elyse Taylor's career.

Now Tori decided her mother looked tense. Could she be nervous about meeting Elyse?

"Did you work on your double axel today?" Mrs. Carsen asked.

Why does she have to pressure me about my skating *now*? Tori thought. Can't she just let it go for once?

Tori didn't answer. Maybe her mother would get the message.

"I asked you a question," Mrs. Carsen said sharply.

Tori sighed. "*Yes,* I worked on my double axel," she snapped.

"Good." Mrs. Carsen didn't seem to notice Tori's tone. "I don't want Elyse to think you're not serious about skating. And the way you've been landing that double axel lately—it really makes you look like a much younger skater. Like a ten-year-old."

"Mom! You promised to stop pressuring me like this!" Tori said angrily.

Mrs. Carsen looked embarrassed. "Sorry," she said. "I'm trying not to be so pushy. But it's hard, Tori. Your skating is so important, and I want nothing but the best for you. If you don't work hard . . ."

She let her voice trail off.

Tori sat silently in the passenger seat, staring out the window. Ever since Tori had had a big talk with her mother at the Regional competition in Lake Placid, Mrs. Carsen had been trying to ease up. But she could still be pretty demanding sometimes. None of the other mothers stood by the rink watching their son or daughter's every move and screaming when they made a mistake. None of the other mothers met regularly with the coaches to discuss their child's career. More than once Tori's mother had humiliated her in front of everyone in Silver Blades by yelling at her or criticizing her skating. The worst part was that no matter how hard she tried to ignore the things her mother said, they still hurt and made Tori feel as if she weren't good enough. Tori had plenty of her own doubts about whether she'd be able to fulfill her dreams and become an Olympic champion. She didn't want her mother adding to the pressure.

As they pulled into the circular driveway, Tori saw another car sitting in front of her modern, split-level stone house. It was a black sports car— a Honda Del Sol. Tori recognized it right away as Blake Michaels's car.

"Hi!" Tori called, jumping out of the car and waving.

Blake climbed out of the driver's side of his car, and a moment later Elyse slid out of the passenger's side.

Tori caught her breath. Tall and graceful, with high cheekbones and silky, shoulder-length auburn hair, Elyse was even more beautiful in person than on TV. She wore large tortoiseshell sunglasses and a white silk parka with white fur trim around the hood. The parka was open slightly, and Tori could see that underneath she had on a black cashmere sweater and white stretch pants with black suede boots. A black leather tote bag was slung over her shoulder.

Tori glanced at her mother. Even *she's* impressed, Tori thought, a bit surprised. Tori's mother was one of the most glamorous people in Seneca Hills, and it took a lot to impress her. But something about Elyse—maybe it was her clothes, or the way she carried herself—forced people—including Mrs. Carsen—to stop and take notice.

"Hi," Elyse said, flashing them her familiar smile. "It is *so* kind of you to have me." She quickly looked around, taking in the large, stylish house and the landscaped grounds. "What a great house! I love the stone wall—especially all covered with snow. It's such a pleasure to be able to stay in a real house instead of another hotel."

Boy, she *is* nice, Tori thought. She's a skating superstar, and here she is, going out of her way to thank us and make us feel at ease.

Blake made some quick introductions, and then Tori's mother took charge.

"I'll bet you're tired, after your flight," Mrs. Carsen said, taking Elyse gently by the arm. "Tori, please give Blake a hand with those bags. I'll show Elyse to her room."

Tori helped Blake carry in the luggage, then

trailed along while Mrs. Carsen gave Elyse a quick tour of the split-level house. Tori was so excited, she could hardly stand it. Elyse Taylor was really here—in her house!

"Here's your room," Mrs. Carsen said, ushering Elyse into the guest room on the top floor.

"It's lovely," Elyse gushed, eyeing the vase of red tulips and the blond Scandinavian furnishings. "Thank you so much."

"You're welcome," Mrs. Carsen said warmly. "I hope you'll make yourself at home."

"I will," Elyse promised. "I already feel so comfortable here."

Mrs. Carsen went downstairs while Tori lingered in the doorway of the room for a few minutes. She was dying to watch Elyse unpack, but she didn't want her to think she was nosy.

Then Elyse glanced over to Tori. "Want to see something?" she asked.

"Definitely!" Tori exclaimed, blushing a little. Had her curiosity about Elyse been that obvious?

Elyse held up her Olympic warm-up jacket and smirked. "Isn't it just the ugliest thing you've ever seen?"

Tori grinned. The Olympic jacket *was* hideous—it had a patchwork of five different red-white-and-blue fabrics, all sewn in stripes. And the warm-up pants were even worse. With wide stripes up and down the legs, the pants reminded her of the kind that clowns on stilts wore in the circus.

Tori laughed. "It's not the best uniform the Olympic committee ever came up with," she agreed.

"No kidding," Elyse said. "Anyway I have to take it with me everywhere, because people want to see me in it." She rolled her eyes.

Tori's surprise at Elyse's less-than-enthusiastic attitude must have shown on her face. Immediately Elyse lowered her voice and reached out for Tori's hand. "Don't tell anyone I said that, okay?"

"Okay," Tori said, shrugging.

Elyse squeezed her hand. "It's so great being around another skater," she said.

Another skater? Elyse's words echoed in Tori's head. Elyse made it sound as if they were close friends, or members of the same skating club.

Tori smiled back at her. "Do you have your gold medal with you?" she asked shyly.

"Of course," Elyse said. She dug around in one of her suitcases until she found a velvet pouch. She loosened the drawstrings and turned the pouch upside down. The gold medal fell onto the bed, gleaming in the light. Elyse handed it to Tori.

A shiver rippled through Tori as she felt the weight of the gold medallion in her hand. She couldn't imagine anything more wonderful than having one of her own. Just holding it was a thrill.

"You wouldn't believe what a crazy night that

was, after the medal ceremony," Elyse said. She sat down on the bed beside Tori. "They had a big party for us, and Betina Metz got so wild! She took off her silver medal and tried to float it in the big fountain outside the hotel. It started to sink, and then she had to jump in after it. She got totally soaked."

Tori giggled. "She must have looked pretty foolish."

Elyse nodded. "I'll say. Lucky for her it was late, and most of the press photographers had gone home."

"She's going to be tough competition in four years," Tori commented, thinking ahead to the next Olympics.

"Oh, please," Elyse said in disgust. "Her spins are *so* slow. And her arms look like sticks. But she's a good jumper. And that's all the judges want these days."

Tori just nodded. She wasn't sure what to say. She thought Betina's spins had looked pretty good during her Olympic program.

Elyse caught Tori staring at her and smiled. "It's such a relief to talk to someone who understands what I've been going through," she said gratefully. "Most people I meet on tour have no idea what the world of skating is really like."

That's true, Tori thought. Elyse probably has to be so careful about what she says in public.

Elyse reached into her black leather tote bag

and pulled out a blue headband with the Olympic symbol on it. She handed it to Tori.

"Here," she said. "I brought this for you. It's an official USA Olympic-team headband."

"Really? For me?"

Elyse nodded.

"Thanks!" Tori said. "That is so nice of you."

"Oh, it's nothing," Elyse said. "I mean, I'm a guest in your house. It's the least I can do. You know, all of a sudden I'm dying of thirst. Do you think you could get me some soda?"

"Sure," Tori said. "I'll be right back."

As she flew down the stairs, her spirit soared. Elyse had only been here a few minutes, and so far things were going great. Elyse was just as nice as everyone said, and she already seemed to think of Tori as a friend.

"It's only a matter of time," Tori murmured to herself gleefully as she poured out two glasses of diet cola and ran back upstairs with them.

Now she was sure she would be able to get Elyse to teach her the layback spin, and get her to talk to Blake about choreographing a new routine for her.

"Jill?" That night Tori sprawled across the bed with the receiver of the phone cradled against her ear.

"Hey, Tori," Jill said. "I'm glad you called. What's up?"

"Oh, nothing," Tori said casually. "Nothing much. Just Elyse Taylor is staying at my house, that's all."

"No! You're kidding!" Jill screamed.

"I'm totally serious." Tori laughed. It was fun having something exciting to tell Jill for a change. Usually Jill was the one who called up with all the cool news. At the Ice Academy she often met top skaters who came to visit or give classes. Plus she ran into interesting people at ice shows and competitions that Silver Blades members didn't attend.

"When did this happen? How? Tell me everything," Jill demanded.

Tori quickly explained how Blake Michaels had just come to Seneca Hills and that he was an old friend of Elyse's. Drawing out every detail, she told Jill all about the famous skater's arrival.

"That's amazing," Jill replied. "Have you had a chance to talk to Elyse yet?"

"This afternoon I hung out in her room, and she gave me an Olympic headband!" Tori bragged. "And she let me hold her gold medal."

"That's so cool," Jill said. "So is she as phony as everyone says?"

"What?" Tori's jaw dropped.

"A lot of the skaters and coaches here know her," Jill explained. "And they say she's not the sweet person she pretends to be on TV. In fact, I heard she's a real ice princess."

An ice princess? Tori thought. Elyse Taylor? She wasn't at all cold or stuck up like some of the skaters Tori thought of as "ice princesses." Elyse was friendly and polite and very generous. Hadn't she just given Tori the Olympic headband?

"That's ridiculous," Tori snapped. "What are you talking about?"

"I'm just telling you what I heard," Jill said.

Tori could feel her face getting hot. Why did Jill have to know everything all the time? Why couldn't Tori be the one to have the inside information for once?

"Really, Jill," Tori began in a haughty tone. "I'm surprised that you'd believe all that gossip you hear about Elyse. I mean, did it ever occur to you that the people who are saying these things are just jealous of her?"

"Well," Jill wavered, "I guess that could be it."

"I'm *sure* that's it," Tori went on. "And if I were you, I wouldn't be so quick to spread ugly rumors about people. Especially when you don't know the truth."

"Fine," Jill said. Then she quickly changed the subject to a party that was coming up in her dorm in a few weeks.

When Tori hung up the phone a few minutes later, she felt a slight pang of regret. She hadn't meant to snap at Jill, but she couldn't stop herself. Having Elyse Taylor as a houseguest was one of the best things that had ever happened to her. She wasn't about to let some nasty rumors ruin things—even if it meant arguing with one of her oldest and closest friends.

4

"**U**mmm." Elyse stretched her arms and arched her back. "That is the most comfortable bed I've ever slept in."

Tori's mother smiled at her from across the kitchen table. "I'm glad you slept well last night, Elyse. But what are you doing up so early—especially after a late night out with Blake? Did Tori wake you?"

Tori scowled at her mother. The Silver Blades skaters practiced twice every weekday—once very early in the morning before school started and then again in the afternoon. This morning when she got up for practice, Tori had tried extra hard to be quiet so as not to wake Elyse.

Elyse pulled her long flowered silk robe around

her more tightly. "No, it wasn't Tori's fault. I guess
I've been waking up so early for so long that I can't
sleep late anymore. My internal alarm clock just
wakes me up." She sniffed the air, then glanced
around the room. "The coffee smells delicious. May
I have some?"

"Of course," Mrs. Carsen said, jumping up to pour
a cup for Elyse.

Elyse took the cup and sniffed the steamy bev-
erage.

"Fabulous," she pronounced. "I swear it's the best
coffee I've ever had."

I wish Jill could be here right now, Tori thought
spitefully. Then she'd see how nice Elyse is—and
how wrong she was to call her an ice princess.

"Tori, you'd better get moving or you're going to
be late," Mrs. Carsen said.

"I'm almost ready," Tori answered.

"Listen," Elyse said. "I'm up and ready to get out
of here. Why don't I drive Tori to her practice this
morning, Mrs. Carsen? And you can stay home and
go back to sleep."

"That would be wonderful," Tori's mother cooed.
"Are you sure?"

"Definitely," Elyse insisted.

"Well, thank you," Mrs. Carsen said. "It's been
ages since I had the opportunity to sleep late. Tori
and I get up at five-thirty every day."

Elyse nodded sympathetically. "It's tough being
a skater's mom."

"Usually I don't mind at all," Mrs. Carsen confessed. "Tori's a very talented skater—one of the best in her club—though if she wants to go anywhere, she's going to have to learn more jumps and spins." She looked at Elyse almost shyly. "Maybe you can show Tori how to do your famous Taylor layback spin."

"Sure," Elyse replied, beaming at Mrs. Carsen. "I should have plenty of time to spend with Tori during the week."

I hope so, Tori thought eagerly.

For once she didn't mind her mother's interference. Having a program choreographed by Blake for the upcoming competition would be great. But learning the Taylor layback would be absolutely perfect. Especially since no one else in Silver Blades had even tried the spin yet. Now she could hardly wait to get on the ice this morning.

"I rented a car in town when Blake and I went out to dinner last night," Elyse told Tori. "It's in the driveway. I'll just run upstairs and throw on some clothes. I'll be ready in a minute."

Tori and her mother looked at each other and smiled.

At least my mother and I have *one* thing in common, Tori thought. We both adore having Elyse Taylor staying in our house!

Tori packed her schoolbooks into her backpack and gathered up her skating bag. Then she checked her outfit in the hall mirror. For practice that morning she was wearing her new silver unitard. Tori knew it looked good with her blue-and-white Silver Blades warm-up jacket. But it was so cold outside, she decided she'd better wear her bright blue down jacket instead.

All bundled up, Tori waited by the back door. When Elyse finally came downstairs, she had on a black cashmere coat and a long pink-and-white flowered silk scarf over her skating clothes. "Ready?" she called.

Tori nodded and opened the door. Sitting in the driveway was a shiny new white sports car.

Cool! Tori thought as she hurried around to the passenger's side. Wait till everyone sees us drive up. She climbed into the small car and buckled up.

"Hey, is there a coffee shop on the way?" Elyse asked as she pulled out of the driveway. "I hardly had time to finish mine. Let's stop and get something warm to drink and a Danish or something to eat."

Tori glanced at her watch. It was five-twenty and the ice rink was exactly ten minutes away. Practice started at five-thirty.

"Uh—there's a doughnut shop that opens early," Tori said, "but we don't have much time. I don't want to be late."

"Don't worry. I'll just dash in and dash out."

Tori pointed the way, and Elyse sped down the still-dark road. By the time she turned into the doughnut-shop parking lot, the clock in the car read five-thirty.

This is going to be fun, Tori told herself, trying to ignore the time. Everyone in the doughnut shop will probably recognize Elyse and make a big fuss over her.

Since winning the medal at the Olympics, the skater had appeared on just about every national TV news show, and her picture had been on the cover of dozens of magazines. How could anyone not recognize Elyse Taylor?

Tori hopped out of the car. As soon as she and Elyse walked into the shop, several heads turned. A number of the regulars were skating parents— mothers and fathers who dropped their kids off at the rink and then grabbed a light breakfast before picking their kids up again and driving them to school. Just as Tori had guessed, there was an immediate stir.

"Elyse Taylor!" Katie Vogel's mother gasped. She jumped up from her seat and rushed over to Tori and Elyse. She grabbed Elyse's hand and squeezed it. "What a pleasure to meet you. I've never seen anyone skate a long program like yours in the Olympics. That spin . . ."

Tori just stood next to Elyse, listening. Mrs. Vogel didn't even notice her. Instead she went on and on about Elyse's program and how thrilling it was to have her here in Seneca Hills.

Then Tori glanced at the clock. Ten minutes had

passed and Elyse still hadn't even ordered her coffee.

Tori tried to get Elyse's attention, but Elyse didn't seem to notice.

"Oh, I'm so happy to be in Seneca Hills," Elyse said to Mrs. Vogel, smiling warmly. "It reminds me of all those years as a young skater. Getting up early on cold, dark winter mornings. Working so hard on my jumps that I'd dream only about axels and toe loops every night. Believe me, these are the best memories a skater will ever have."

Mrs. Vogel laughed and shook her head. "Well, they aren't the best memories a skating *mom* will ever have, I can tell you that!"

Tori cleared her throat. "Uh, Elyse, did you want to order some coffee?" she asked anxiously. "We've got to go."

"In a minute." Elyse sounded irritated. "I'm having a conversation."

Just then Patrick McGuire's father hopped off his stool at the counter and came over to Elyse. After introducing himself, he pulled a business card out of his wallet and started talking to Elyse about the T-shirt company he owned. Tori shifted on her feet nervously while Mr. McGuire tried to convince Elyse that she should let him print up 500 T-shirts that would say ELYSE TAYLOR IN SENECA HILLS for the skating benefit next Sunday night.

Tori stood by while Elyse talked to three more parents and signed autographs. By the time they left the doughnut shop, it was six o'clock. Tori was going to be more than half an hour late.

She climbed silently into the car, trying to hide her annoyance.

"Sorry I got so carried away in there," Elyse said breezily.

"Yeah. Well, that's okay," Tori replied. "I just hate to be late for practice."

"I *said* I was sorry," Elyse snapped. Then her voice softened again. "Listen, I'll make it up to you tonight, if I can. Think of a nice place to eat, and I'll take you out to dinner after your afternoon skating practice—if I can get away. Okay?"

"Sure." As Tori gave the skater a big smile, she felt her anger melt. Having dinner with Elyse would be so much fun. Maybe she'd also get a chance to talk about having Blake choreograph a program for her.

"Tori! You're not concentrating!" Mr. Weiler said as Tori fell out of a double toe loop. Tori got up and skated toward her coach, who was standing at the far corner of the ice.

How am I supposed to concentrate with so much going on? Tori wondered. Having Elyse Taylor at her house was exciting, but it was distracting, too. She'd been in such a hurry to get on the ice this morning, she'd rushed her warm-up and caught her toe pick on a hole in the ice. With everyone watching, she'd sprawled onto the ice and bruised her knees badly.

So far, this afternoon wasn't going much better. She hadn't landed a single jump.

As Tori skated past Danielle and Nikki, she noticed that her friends were talking to Blake Michaels by the boards. Suddenly her jaw dropped. Danielle was handing him a big chocolate cake.

I can't believe it, Tori thought. Dani baked him a cake! Talk about trying to *butter* him up!

Then Nikki gave Blake a huge card. Tori heard Nikki saying, "My skating partner, Alex Beekman, and I just wanted to find a way to say 'Welcome to Silver Blades.' "

I can't believe it, Tori thought. My best friends are plotting ways to win over Blake Michaels—behind my back!

"Tori? Are you listening to me?" Mr. Weiler's voice broke through Tori's thoughts. As she skated up to him, he shook his head. "No, don't even answer. I can see that you aren't really with us today. That's enough for now. We'll work on your program again tomorrow."

Tori cringed. Mr. Weiler rarely yelled or spoke harshly the way Kathy did, but in his quiet ways he let his feelings be known just as clearly. And Tori hated to disappoint him. She knew she was lucky to have the chance to train under Franz Weiler. He was a well-known and highly respected coach.

"Sorry," Tori said quietly before Mr. Weiler skated away. "I'll be more prepared in the morning."

Tori hurried into the locker room and found Nikki and Danielle already changing out of their practice clothes. It was the first time she'd had a chance to talk to them all day. She'd been too late to practice this morning to have time to chat with anyone, and she and her friends went to separate schools. Nikki and Danielle attended the public school in Seneca Hills, while Tori went to Kent Academy, a private school in a nearby town.

"Tori! Hi!" Nikki said. "Get over here immediately and tell us *everything* about Elyse."

"Where were you this morning, anyway?" Danielle asked. "You were so late for practice."

"Oh, uh, well, Elyse and I went out for coffee," Tori said, trying to make it sound like it was no big deal. "And we were having so much fun, we just got carried away. You know—talking about skating and stuff. I guess we just lost track of time."

It wasn't a total lie, but it wasn't exactly the truth either. Besides, Tori told herself, it's not like the two of them told me about their plans to give Blake a cake and a card. Tori sat down on the bench without looking at Nikki and Danielle and started to take off her skates.

"Well?" Danielle asked. "What's she like? Is she nice? Does she really eat a lot? Is she as beautiful in person?"

Tori laughed at the flood of questions. "Of course

she's nice," she began. "I mean, you've seen her on TV. She's really generous, too. She gave me an Olympic headband and let me try on her gold medal."

"That's so cool!" Nikki exclaimed. "You got to wear her medal?"

Tori nodded. "It was great." She tossed her head. "I think I'm the only person she's let wear it."

"Wow," Danielle breathed. "So what else happened? Did you hang out with her last night?"

"Well . . ." Tori hesitated. She couldn't very well tell them that Elyse had gone out with Blake and hadn't come back until after midnight, after Tori was asleep.

"She and I stayed up all night talking about the Olympics," Tori lied. "She let me try on some of her clothes, too. She has an incredible wardrobe. Practically everything she wears is either cashmere or silk."

"Can we come over and talk to her sometime?" Nikki asked.

"Oh, sure," Tori said. "I'm just not sure when."

Not before I have a chance to talk to Elyse about Blake, Tori vowed silently. *I* have to be the next one to work with him. I just have to be.

Haley entered the locker room wearing a black sweatshirt and red spandex biking shorts over black tights. As usual she looked more like a street hockey player or a kid on Rollerblades than a figure skater. She pulled her skating bag out of her locker and quickly changed out of her skates into black high-top sneakers.

"Hey—who wants to go to the mall?" Haley asked.

"On a school night?" Danielle asked. Her friends grinned. Danielle was well known for getting good grades and making sure her homework was done on time.

"Sure," Haley said. "Just for a while. We can get a pizza maybe. I was talking to the guys, and they're all going to be there. Jordan's mom is going to drive."

Tori knew what that meant. When Haley said "the guys," she was referring to a group of eighth-grade hockey players—Kyle Dorset, who was Nikki's boyfriend; Nicolas Panati, who was Danielle's older brother; and Jordan McShane, the eighth-grader Danielle liked. Alex Beekman usually hung out with them too.

Nikki's face lit up. "Kyle's going? I think my mother will let me go," she said quickly. "As long as we don't stay out late. She falls asleep really early these days since she's pregnant."

"Actually I can go, too," Danielle said. "I don't have much homework this week."

Haley laughed. "I thought I could talk you into it," she said. "Especially when you heard Jordan was going."

"Well, count me out," Tori announced. "I'd love to come, but I'm going out to dinner with Elyse. She's picking me up here."

"Really?" Haley looked surprised. "Because she left here about an hour ago to get a manicure. And she told Blake that she wouldn't be back."

"What?" Tori said, dumbfounded.

"I overheard them talking. Blake was working on the new program with Patrick and me," Haley explained. "You wouldn't believe how great the program is, by the way. Blake is a major talent, for sure. Then Elyse stopped by and said she had an appointment."

"Oh." Tori felt her face growing red. She reached down to tie the laces on her running shoes, letting her hair fall forward so that it partially covered her face.

I can't believe she forgot about our dinner date, Tori thought. How *could* she? Elyse hadn't remembered to work with Tori on the spin either.

She forced herself to look up at her friends. "I guess I got confused about which night we're supposed to go out," she said with a shrug. "Elyse explained her whole schedule to me, and I could hardly keep up with it."

"So you *can* come with us, then," Nikki said warmly.

"Right." Tori nodded, feeling herself recover quickly. "And it's a good thing, too. I'll probably be spending so much time with Elyse, this will be my last chance to hang out with you guys all week."

Danielle sighed. "You're so lucky, Tori."

"I know," Tori told her friend emphatically. "It's so cool having Elyse Taylor for a friend."

5

"She's amazing," Nikki said under her breath.

"I know," Tori agreed, staring in awe as Elyse glided across the ice.

It was Wednesday afternoon, and Tori and her friends sat together in the seats surrounding the figure-skating rink. On the ice Elyse Taylor was teaching a class of the youngest skaters in Silver Blades.

Tori watched, spellbound by Elyse's grace. Flawlessly the skater leaned forward onto the outside edge of her left skate, arched her back, lifted her right leg behind her until it was higher than her head, and began the long, graceful move known as a spiral. Her navy-blue satin skating dress shimmered and rippled in the breeze created by her own speed.

The faces of the youngest skaters were glowing with excitement.

"The important thing to remember is to keep your right leg straight and perfectly still," Elyse instructed as she demonstrated the spiral again. "Don't let it droop."

"I can't believe we're actually sitting here watching her teach a class at Seneca Hills Ice Arena," Nikki said with a sigh. She glanced at Tori. "And I still can't believe she's staying at your house. Aren't you in total awe?"

Tori smiled at her friend and shrugged. "I'm starting to get used to it," she said quickly. "After all, it's been three days already." She pointed to the ice, where Elyse was demonstrating a jump combination. "How come I can't make my combinations look smooth?"

To Tori's relief Nikki looked back at the rink, and the subject of Elyse was dropped. Tori didn't want her friends to know the truth, which was that so far Elyse hadn't spent very much time at all in the Carsen home. Most of the time she went out with Blake or shopping at the mall. And when she was home, all she did was drink their gourmet coffee and sleep.

Then Danielle leaned closer to Tori. "What's with Elyse and Blake, anyway? I mean, are they a couple or what?"

Tori hated to admit that she didn't know. Especially after she'd bragged to her friends that Elyse told her all her secrets.

"She doesn't really want me to talk about that," Tori said, pulling back from Danielle a little.

Danielle leaned back against the bleachers with a hurt expression.

Tori's face reddened. She hadn't meant to hurt her friend's feelings. But what else could she say?

"Check that out!" Haley's voice was filled with admiration. "Elyse just landed three flawless triple flips in a row!"

"That's what it takes to be a champion," Tori said.

Haley turned to Tori. "But I was right about her, wasn't I, Tori? She's not really very nice in person. I heard her talking to Blake, and she was sort of nasty. Her little-miss-perfect thing is just an act, isn't it?"

"That's not true," Tori protested. "She practically treats me like a sister. She even gave me this pair of earrings, see?"

Tori twisted her head sideways and pulled back her hair so that her friends could see the small silver earrings. They were round disks, with tiny white enamel skates on them.

"Those are so pretty," Nikki said.

"Aren't they great?" Tori let her hair drop to cover her ears again.

Why did I just do that? she asked herself. She hadn't meant to lie. It had just slipped out. Elyse hadn't given her the earrings—Tori's mother had bought them for her during a business trip to New York the previous week.

"Maybe she has a split personality," Haley joked. "Like Dr. Jekyll and Mr. Hyde. Maybe she's really nice—but only when she's around *you*, Tori. And then she's obnoxious the rest of the time—like when she orders Blake to take her out to dinner every night."

Nikki and Danielle laughed at Haley's joke.

Then Danielle nodded. "Last night Jill told me all this stuff about Elyse . . ." She turned expectantly to look at Tori.

"Jill shouldn't spread rumors," Tori replied tartly.

"I don't think they were rumors," Danielle began. "She said she heard—"

Abruptly Tori stood up. "I can't believe Jill," she said indignantly, cutting Danielle off midsentence. "Before she started at the Academy, she wasn't the kind of person who gossiped about people she'd never met."

Nikki opened her mouth to reply, but before she could say anything, Tori marched out of the bleachers.

How can they say those things? she thought, growing more furious by the minute. Dani, Haley, and Jill are acting as if they know Elyse better than I do— even though Elyse is staying at *my* house!

Tori brushed past Kathy and Mr. Weiler, who stood at the end of the ice rink watching Elyse from behind the barrier.

"Leaving so soon?" Kathy called to Tori.

"I don't feel well," Tori replied.

"Oh. I'm sorry to hear that," Kathy said.

Mr. Weiler raised his eyebrows. "Are you going to miss practice?"

"No," Tori answered quickly. "I'm just going to lie down in the locker room for a few minutes."

"By the way," Kathy called after Tori, "how are you enjoying my Margo DeForest book?"

Tori froze. With all the excitement of Elyse's visit she had forgotten all about the book.

"Uh, it's great," Tori said, fumbling for words. "But, um, I haven't gotten very far yet. May I keep it another few days?"

"Of course," Kathy said. "Just be careful with it. It's one of my most prized possessions, and I'd like it back before the end of the week."

"No problem," Tori replied, resolving to pick up the book again as soon as she got home.

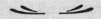

By the time Tori finished her own practice session that afternoon, it was nearly six o'clock, and Elyse was already gone. She had offered to give Tori a ride home, but instead of waiting for Tori she left the rink right after teaching her class.

Tori was standing in line at the pay phone to call her mother when Haley spotted her.

"Need a ride home?" Haley called. Tori nodded,

and Haley pointed outside. "My mom's already here. Come on."

As Tori climbed into Mrs. Arthur's car, she couldn't help feeling embarrassed about her angry outburst in the bleachers earlier. Haley was a good friend—so were Nikki and Dani. Why had she gotten so angry with them over Elyse?

To Tori's relief Haley seemed to have forgotten all about the incident, and chattered nonstop the whole way home. By the time Haley's mother pulled up at the curb in front of Tori's house, Tori resolved to be extra nice to her friends tomorrow. She couldn't exactly take back her sharp words, but she could try to make up for them.

The house smelled of garlic and basil when Tori opened the kitchen door at her house.

"You're so late," Tori's mother said as she chopped yellow peppers for a salad.

"I'm starved. And exhausted," Tori said. "Do I have time to soak in a hot tub before dinner?"

"Sure," Mrs. Carsen said. Then she glanced toward the stairway and lowered her voice. "Elyse hasn't said a word since she came in. And I thought she was driving you home. Is everything okay?"

"How would I know?" Tori answered with a shrug. "I got a ride with Mrs. Arthur."

"Did you get Elyse to teach you the Taylor layback yet?" Tori's mother pressed her.

"Not yet."

"Well, you'd better talk to her about it soon," Mrs.

Carsen said. "And try to get her to talk to Blake for you, too. Maybe she can get him to choreograph a program for you next."

Yeah, right, Tori thought as she ran up the stairs to her room. I can't even get Elyse to wait for me after practice, let alone teach me the layback or talk Blake into working with me. What does Mom expect from me—miracles?

Tori filled the bathtub with hot water and bubble bath, and climbed in. Twenty minutes later she felt warm and relaxed. She put on a comfortable outfit—red knit pants and a gray sweater with red buttons. Then she poked her head into the guest room across the hall, trying to summon up the courage to ask Elyse why she hadn't waited for her after practice.

The famous skater was lying on top of the comforter reading a book. Tori tilted her head sideways to see the book's spine. Then it hit her. The faded red cover. The old, worn binding. It was Kathy's book!

What nerve, Tori thought. Elyse had obviously gone into Tori's room and taken the book from her desk.

"Is that my book?" she blurted out.

"Oh, hi!" Elyse said brightly. "I hope you don't mind that I borrowed it. I was bored to death when I got home from the rink, and this was all I could find to do."

Tori hesitated. "I guess it's okay," she said. "But Kathy . . ."

Before Tori could finish, Elyse turned her attention back to the page in front of her.

"Kathy Bart needs—" Tori tried again, but Elyse
cut her off.

"Can't it wait? I'm reading right now," Elyse said
without looking up.

"Never mind." Tori retreated into the hallway and
stood there for a few minutes.

I can't believe she's treating me like this, she
thought. And I can't believe I'm taking it. Just then
Tori's mother came up the stairs and stopped in
the hall.

"What's she doing?" Mrs. Carsen whispered.

"Reading," Tori said.

Mrs. Carsen knocked softly on the guest-room
door. It was still standing ajar.

"I said I'm *reading* now!" Elyse's voice was filled
with irritation.

"I'm sorry, Elyse," Mrs. Carsen said, "but I just
wanted to let you know that dinner will be ready in
about five minutes."

"Oh!" Elyse looked up, surprised. "I didn't realize
it was you. Dinner? Oh, no, I've got to get dressed.
I'm going to meet Blake for dinner tonight."

"But—" Mrs. Carsen sputtered the word. "I thought
you'd eat with us."

Elyse must have noticed the look of disappoint-
ment on Mrs. Carsen's face. Instantly she turned on
her charm. "Oh, I'm sorry," she said. "I should have
told you not to expect me for meals. I mean, it's bad

enough that I'm staying in your house, imposing on you like this. I just couldn't expect you to cook for me, too."

"It's no trouble," Mrs. Carsen said. "Really. Maybe Blake would like to join us? You could call him and—"

"Oh, no," Elyse interrupted. "I don't even know where to reach him right now. I'm meeting him downtown in the lobby of the Circle Tower Hotel."

She jumped up and began racing around the room, getting ready to leave.

On the way out of the room Elyse grabbed her coat and picked up Kathy's book. "Blake is always late," she said, rolling her eyes at Tori. "I think I'll take this book along to read while I'm waiting for him."

"Uh," Tori said, panicking, "you can't. I mean, I'm sorry, but it's not my book. I can't let you borrow it. That's what I was trying to tell you."

Elyse looked at Tori with a snotty expression.

"Are you kidding? It's just a book."

"Yes, but it's not mine, and it's very old and valuable, and—"

"Don't be a baby," Elyse said as she pushed past Tori. "It's just a stupid book. What do you think I'm going to do? Lose it?"

Then she dashed down the stairs and out the door with the book in her hands, before Tori could say another word.

6

Tori peered out her bedroom window early the next morning. The full moon was still shining brightly across a light layer of new snow on the front lawn. Shivering in the early-morning cold, Tori pulled on leggings and a sweatshirt, then tiptoed across the hall to peek into the guest room.

So much for your internal clock waking you up early, Elyse, Tori thought. She stared at the sleeping skater, whose auburn hair was fanned across the pillow. Even in her sleep Elyse looked beautiful and elegant—like a star.

Tori pushed open the door a little farther and slipped into the room. Where is it? Tori wondered, scanning the room for Kathy's book. She would feel a lot better once she had it in her own hands. But the book was nowhere in sight.

At this rate I'll *never* get to finish it, Tori thought. Maybe Kathy wouldn't ask her about it again today. It would be so embarrassing to have to admit that she hadn't read another word.

Tori tiptoed out of the room and headed downstairs to make herself a quick bowl of microwave oatmeal. Then she packed up her gear and piled into her mother's car, hoping to catch an extra ten minutes of sleep on the way to the rink.

Inside the locker room at the Ice Arena Nikki and Danielle were both sitting on benches lacing up their skates. When Tori walked in, neither of them looked at her or said a word. Haley might have forgiven her for yesterday, but obviously these two were still angry.

"Hi," Tori said, breaking the silence. "Listen, I'm sorry about yesterday. I don't know why I lost it like that. I guess I'm just sort of tense."

"That's okay," Nikki replied quickly.

"Yeah," Danielle agreed, smiling. "Forget it."

Relief washed over Tori. She hated arguing with her friends.

"Haley and Patrick are already on the ice," Nikki told Tori. "Can you believe it? They're so psyched about the program Blake is doing for them, they came at five o'clock to work on it."

"That's great," Tori said.

"I don't mean to bring up a sore subject," Danielle began. "But I thought Elyse was going to spend a whole week giving classes at the arena. But when she's here, all she does is work on her own routine. And why haven't you invited us over so we can watch her every move? Huh? Are you trying to keep her all to yourself, or what?"

Tori laughed. It felt good to have her friends joking with her again. "Elyse has been pretty busy," she said truthfully. She remembered her vow to make things up to Dani, Nikki, and Haley. "How about this afternoon? After practice—are you guys free? Maybe you can come over for dinner."

"I can't," Nikki said.

"Why not?

"Well, first I want to watch the group class with Elyse."

"I almost forgot about that," Tori said.

"I'll be there, too," Danielle added. "*If* Elyse shows up."

"Right," Nikki agreed, rolling her eyes. "And then Blake asked Alex and me to stay late today, to show him our program."

Tori felt a ripple of jealousy run through her. "He did? Why?"

"I'm not sure," Nikki said, sounding excited. "But I've got my fingers crossed. Maybe he's going to choreograph programs for all the pairs!"

Oh, great, Tori thought. This probably means he's going to choose Nikki and Alex to work with next! This is the thanks I get for asking her and Dani to come over.

Tori bent down and finished lacing her skates in

silence while Nikki and Danielle each mentioned how she hoped Blake would choose to work with her next.

Not if I can help it, Tori thought. The next skater to get a Blake Michaels routine is going to be Tori Carsen.

A cold blast of air hit Tori in the face as she walked into the skating rink that afternoon for the big group lesson with Elyse. She had initially forgotten about today's special session, but now she was ready. Tori had on one of her favorite skating dresses. It had a silver bodice with gray chiffon sleeves and two layers of white and gray chiffon skirts.

Blake Michaels stood near the barrier as Tori stepped onto the ice.

"Wow!" he whistled, eyeing her outfit. "Go get 'em, Tori."

Tori smiled and blushed. At least he noticed me, she thought as she circled the ice, warming up.

Within a few minutes Tori was sharing the ice with four other skaters. Danielle warmed up with simple jumps, wearing her usual outfit—a baggy bright-colored T-shirt and leggings.

Diana Mitchell, the oldest and most accomplished skater in Silver Blades, practiced her sit-spins in a corner. At sixteen years old Diana competed in the senior women's division. She usually wore her bright-red hair either loose or in a ponytail for practices, but today she had it in a French braid. She'd also chosen to wear one of her nicest skating dresses, a rust-colored velvet dress trimmed in gold braid. Obviously Tori wasn't the only one interested in impressing Blake Michaels and Elyse Taylor.

Two other skaters, Sara Russell and Christine Rosenblum, both twelve years old, did several waltz jumps in a large circle to warm up.

Haley and her partner, Patrick, sat in the bleachers with Nikki and Alex. As pairs skaters they weren't part of this lesson, but they wanted to watch Elyse every minute they could.

Tori's mother and a dozen other skating parents sat a few rows away drinking coffee out of thermoses. Everyone in Seneca Hills wants to watch Elyse, Tori realized.

Even some of the hockey players had shown up to see the famous figure skater teach. Kyle, Nikki's boyfriend, sat next to Nikki, leaning awkwardly on his elbows with his chin in his hands.

Finally Elyse strolled out of the locker room. Tori was sure that she had deliberately waited until all the other girls finished changing so that she could have some privacy.

Now Elyse stood at the entrance to the rink dressed in a sleek metallic-blue unitard with silver stripes, and removed her rubber skate guards.

"Elyse, you look almost as beautiful as Tori," Blake teased.

Tori blushed again and smiled at Elyse. But Elyse didn't look in Tori's direction.

"Thanks *so* much," Elyse said, smiling, but Tori could tell that Blake had just said the wrong thing.

Blake laughed, and Elyse flashed him a look that could burn holes through the ice.

Then she stepped onto the rink and skated around for a few minutes to warm up.

"Okay," she said finally as she skidded to a stop, spraying ice. "Let's get started."

Tori, Danielle, Diana, Christine, and Sara gathered around.

"Why don't we start with the loop?" Elyse suggested. "Has anyone here mastered the triple yet?"

Everyone laughed, even Diana. The loop was a hard jump because the skater had to launch herself into the air on the back outside edge of the skate blade without using her free leg to help. Not many skaters could do a *triple* loop. Tori knew that even most Olympic skaters had trouble with it.

"Tori, you seem to be one of Blake's favorite skaters here in Seneca Hills," Elyse said in a teasing voice. "Let's see what you can do with the *double* loop." She cocked her head.

Tori flinched. Is she kidding? she thought. Tori had only started landing her double loop a few weeks before, and she definitely hadn't mastered it yet.

Taking a deep breath, Tori skated around the rink

a few times to build up some speed. Then she did a three-turn—which positioned her onto her left foot, while skating backward. A moment later she stepped onto her right skate, then bent her right leg and leaped into the air. But her timing was off. She barely made one and a half turns before landing.

Elyse smiled at the other skaters. "I know I'm staying at Tori's house this week," she said, "but she didn't learn that move from me, I swear."

Diana laughed nervously. So did one or two of the other skaters.

Danielle offered Tori a sympathetic glance, but Tori wanted to sink into the ice and die.

"All right, how about someone else?" Elyse asked. She turned on her magic smile and surveyed the other girls. "How about you?" She pointed at Danielle. "What's your name?"

"Danielle."

"Great, Danielle. Let's see what you can do with the double loop."

Dani rubbed her hands together and then skated forward nervously. Tori could tell from the way Danielle hardly dug into the ice that her friend was tense, and the tension kept her from getting much power in her strokes.

She started to circle the rink, but then stopped. She did a quick turn, coming back to face Elyse.

"Uh, to tell you the truth, I haven't worked on my double loop much at all," she admitted, her voice shaking.

Elyse gave her a warm smile. "That's okay, Danielle. I appreciate your honesty. So what's your best jump?"

"My double salchow," Dani said.

"Fine," Elyse said. "Then why don't we all work on the double salchow together."

For the next forty-five minutes Elyse worked with each girl on the jump. But throughout the whole lesson Elyse encouraged four of the skaters—and picked on Tori nonstop.

"Is that all the height you can get?" she shrieked at her from across the ice. "How long did you say you'd been skating?"

By the end of the lesson Tori's face was burning with shame. She'd never felt so humiliated. Elyse had been yelling at her with the bleachers full of people. And she was sure her mother would tell her she hadn't tried hard enough as soon as she got off the ice.

But the worst part was that Blake Michaels had been standing near the boards watching and listening to the whole thing. Now he'd never choose to work with Tori next. He probably thought she was a terrible skater with no talent at all.

At last Elyse announced that she had to leave. "But you're all doing so much better. I can see an improvement in *almost* everyone."

As the members of Silver Blades started to skate off the ice, Elyse grabbed Tori's arm and held her back. On her face was her usual radiant smile. But Elyse's words cut through Tori like shards of ice.

"Just try to remember," she snarled. "Having beautiful skating clothes won't make up for a life-time of hard work."

Then, as applause from the bleachers filled the arena, Elyse bowed low and waved to the crowd before leaving the ice.

As she skated off behind Elyse, tears welled up in Tori's eyes. Jill was absolutely right, she thought. Elyse might seem friendly and nice, but underneath that sweet act she's the complete opposite—a cold and nasty ice princess.

7

Tori leaned back on a pile of pillows on her bed and cradled the telephone by her ear.

"I can't believe she treated me that way this afternoon," she murmured to Nikki, who listened on the other end of the line.

"Me either," Nikki agreed. "Dani and Haley and I were all mortified for you. I mean, she really picked on you. How come?"

"I don't know," Tori said truthfully. "Blake complimented me on my skating dress, but I can't believe she'd get jealous over that. I mean, he's ten years older than me."

"But is she like that at your house? I thought you said she treated you like a sister."

Tori hesitated. Should she tell Nikki how Elyse *really* acted?

No, Tori decided. Then she'll know I've been lying all along.

"She does treat me like a sister," Tori responded quickly. "That's why I was so surprised. She must have been tired or something today."

"If you say so." Nikki sounded doubtful.

Tori sighed inwardly. It was hard to keep up the act—to keep pretending that Elyse was really nice, when she wasn't. But she'd told so many lies about Elyse that it was hard to admit the truth.

Abruptly Tori sat up in bed and looked toward the hall. "Hey, I think I just heard someone coming up the stairs. I've got to go. Elyse must be home, and there's something I want to talk to her about."

"Okay," Nikki said. "But don't let her push you around. Okay?"

"Okay," Tori said. "And thanks."

Tori hung up quickly and raced out into the hall. But Elyse had already gone into the guest room and closed the door behind her.

Tori knocked on the door. The last thing she wanted to do right now was talk to Elyse. But she had to get Kathy's book back from her.

A deep sigh came from inside the room before Elyse said, "Come in."

"Are you busy?" Tori asked, realizing right away that it was a stupid question.

"Do I *look* busy?" Elyse snapped.

"No. I mean, I don't know," Tori stammered.

Elyse shifted her weight onto her left hip and barely stifled another sigh.

"I wanted to ask you to return my book," Tori said. "The autobiography of Margo DeForest. I need it back."

Elyse spun around and started changing into a nightgown, throwing her clothes in a heap on the floor.

"Actually I am busy," Elyse said. "And I'm exhausted. This is the most tiring trip I've ever been on. Could we talk about this some other time?"

From the tone of her voice and the way Elyse was bustling around the room, Tori could tell that it wasn't a question. It was a statement. Elyse was not about to talk with Tori about the book.

Tori gritted her teeth. She was determined to get what she came for.

"I'm sorry, but I've got to have the book back now," she said. "It doesn't belong to me."

Elyse picked up one of her silk shirts and hurled it onto the bed. "This is ridiculous. I want to get some sleep!" she yelled. "I *knew* I should have stayed at a hotel. I told Blake that from the beginning. At least there I'd have some shred of privacy!"

Tori's mouth fell open. She'd never seen anyone get so angry about something that seemed so trivial.

But almost instantly Elyse seemed to regret her temper.

"Look, I'm sorry," she said. "I'm just way too tired.

Let me get some sleep, and I'll make this up to you tomorrow, okay?"

"Yeah, right," Tori said coldly.

"No, honestly," Elyse said. "Tomorrow is a school holiday, isn't it? Why don't you invite your friends over, and I'll take you all to lunch."

Tori stared at her. She'd heard this before—the time Elyse had promised to take her out to dinner.

"Come on," Elyse coaxed her. "We'll all dress up and go to that fancy place, what's it called? The revolving restaurant—the Circle View—at the top of the Circle Tower Hotel. Maybe I'll see if Blake can join us."

Tori could feel her resolve melting away. She'd given up on Elyse's ever talking to Blake for her, but maybe at lunch Tori would have a chance to talk to Blake personally about choreography for her new routine.

"Really?" Tori said. "You mean it?"

"Yes. Really!" Elyse said with a laugh. "Now, please, let me get some sleep, okay? I'll be grateful forever."

Tori hurried out of the room and closed the door.

I guess I can wait till tomorrow for the book, she decided. It's only one more day. . .

"What time did she say she'd be back?" Haley asked, looking at her watch for the fiftieth time.

"Noon," Tori moaned. "She promised she'd be here with Blake by noon."

"My stomach's growling," Danielle complained. "It's almost one o'clock."

"What a way to waste our day off from school!" Haley said.

Tori didn't know what to say. Once again Elyse had left her feeling angry and embarrassed. Nikki, Haley, and Danielle were being nice about it, but Tori knew they were mad, too. They'd all gotten dressed up and looked fantastic. Nikki had on a Victorian-looking brown jumper with a white lace blouse and white tights. Danielle wore her favorite long red woolen skirt with black boots and an oversized long black sweater. Even Haley was dressed up—sort of. She had on a black leather skirt, a white sweater with lots of zippers on it, and a black leather bomber jacket. This was the first time Tori had ever seen Haley in a skirt.

Tori herself had on a new dress her mother had just bought for her—it was dark green with long sleeves and pearl buttons.

How could Elyse stand them up like this? she wondered. Tori felt like a fool for ever believing her in the first place.

"Let's pre-eat," she suggested, jumping up and heading for the kitchen. "That's what my mom always does when she goes to dinner parties. Her friends never serve dinner until really late."

"Hurry!" Danielle joked. "I think I'm going to faint."

"I'm starved, too," Haley said. "Bring lots."

Tori prepared a tray full of fruit and crackers spread with peanut butter and brought it into the living room. Within a few minutes her friends managed to devour all the snacks.

"Where could Elyse be?" Haley asked, wiping her fingers on a napkin. "I know you said she's gone a lot of the time. But she doesn't know anyone in Seneca Hills except Blake, does she?"

"I don't know," Tori replied with a shrug. "Maybe she went to the rink."

"I doubt it," Haley said. "She has that big rehearsal for the benefit tonight. Plus she was already there this morning. Didn't you hear her?"

Tori shook her head.

"She yelled at Mack for about fifteen minutes," Haley explained.

Tori winced. Everyone loved Mack. He was the sweet old guy who drove the huge tractorlike machine called the Zamboni. It was used to clean and smooth the ice.

"Should we call the rink?" Nikki suggested. "We could ask Toby in the pro shop if he's seen her around."

"No. Let's just go see if her skates are here," Tori said.

She hopped up and headed for the stairs. Her friends followed instantly.

Tori opened the door to the guest room and entered slowly.

"What a mess!" Haley said. "You didn't tell us she was a slob."

Tori looked around at the piles of clothes lying on chairs, on the floor, and on the unmade bed. "I guess I've gotten used to it already," she said.

"Hey, look at this," Nikki said, pointing to a large blue leather scrapbook on the dresser.

Haley glanced around with a guilty expression, then picked up the scrapbook. No one tried to stop her as she flipped it open.

Tori peered over her friend's shoulder. The first few pages had pictures of Elyse as a little girl winning local skating contests. Then there were photos showing Elyse posing with other skaters at National and World skating events.

Danielle leaned in closer and pointed to a picture of Elyse and Blake. In the picture Blake had his arm around Elyse's shoulders. They were dressed up—and from the enormous smiles on their faces it looked as if they were having a great time together.

"Wow," Danielle said. "They look so lovey-dovey. Do you think they were going out together?"

"It seems like it," Tori admitted slowly. "But from the way he teases her and a couple of comments he's made, I get the feeling that he isn't in love with her anymore. I think he just wants to be friends."

"Look!" Haley screamed, pointing to another page of the scrapbook. "I *knew* she was an ice princess at heart! She's written catty comments under all these pictures of other skaters!"

Tori and the others huddled around Haley.

"Listen to this. She wrote 'Ugliest Costume Award to Katya Schmidt—Perfect six-point-oh.'"

Tori looked over Haley's shoulder at the picture.

"That *was* a pretty ugly costume," Tori agreed. "I mean, who wears ruffles like that. She looked like—" She stopped herself as her friends giggled, then looked away.

I sound like Elyse, Tori realized.

Sometimes nasty remarks spilled out of her before she realized what she was saying or was able to stop them.

"Are Elyse's skates here?" Nikki asked suddenly, moving away from the scrapbook. "We didn't come in here to snoop around, you guys. We came to check if her skates are gone."

"I don't see them," Tori answered. "But I'll keep looking."

Tori slid open the door to the closet and scanned the floor. Elyse's skating bag wasn't there. Then she stood on her tiptoes and checked out the closet shelf. Nothing.

She searched under the bed, through the pile of clothes on the chair and the heap on the floor. Tori didn't really expect to find skates in any of those places, but she was also hoping to come across something else—Kathy's book.

There was no sign of it anywhere.

Just then Nikki gasped. "Look!"

"What?" Everyone turned around and caught

Nikki standing frozen, staring at something on the nightstand beside Elyse's bed.

"Is that what I think it is?" Nikki asked, her voice rising.

Tori looked and saw that Nikki was pointing to the velvet pouch that Elyse had shown her a few days earlier—the one with the Olympic gold medal in it. A tiny bit of the red-white-and-blue ribbon was sticking out of the pouch. To any skater who dreamed about winning a medal one day, that ribbon was immediately recognizable.

Tori nodded. "That's her gold medal."

She hesitated for a moment. Her friends were obviously dying to see it. What could it hurt to let them? After all, Elyse had let Tori try it on. And she had acted as though it wasn't such a big deal.

Tori lifted the pouch and spilled the gold medal into her palm.

"Here," she said, handing it to Nikki. "Try it on."

Nikki grinned, then bowed her head solemnly for Tori to drape the medal around her neck.

Tori spoke into an imaginary microphone. "For the United States, the gold medal goes to Nikki Simon!" she announced.

"Yay!" Haley and Danielle yelled, clapping.

For the next five minutes the four girls took turns trying on the gold medal and dancing around the room. When Haley's turn came, she grabbed a hairbrush for her microphone.

"I want to thank all my friends in Silver Blades,"

she said in a syrupy imitation of Elyse. "And let them know that I just want to give something back to all the people who helped me over the years. That's why I'm giving them"—Haley looked around the room frantically and then finally gave up—"this hairbrush!" she said, laughing.

Everyone else burst out laughing, too.

Then Nikki grabbed the hairbrush from Haley and spoke into it. "Well, I want to thank Elyse Taylor for showing me what an ice princess is," Nikki said. "She's taught me what I *don't* want to become when I'm an Olympic champion."

As the other girls giggled, Tori remained quiet. None of her friends had any respect left for Elyse Taylor. And why should they? She'd issued an invitation, then neglected to live up to her promise. There was nothing about Elyse's behavior that deserved their respect or admiration.

But Tori couldn't help feeling as if it were her fault, too. As if she had also let her friends down somehow.

"I'm starved," Haley announced suddenly, interrupting her thoughts. "I say we go to the Circle View Restaurant anyway. I'll call my mom and get her to drive."

"But it's so expensive." Dani hesitated.

"That's okay," Tori said quickly. "We don't have to go there. Let's go to the mall for lunch instead. My treat."

"Really? Thanks!" Dani said.

Tori's friends hurried across the hall into Tori's room to use the phone and call their parents. But Tori lingered behind in the guest room for a moment. She might have given up on Elyse Taylor, but there was still one thing Tori needed from her. She cast her eyes about the room one last time. What had Elyse done with Kathy's book?

8

"Tori, you're not listening to me."

Tori rolled her eyes and turned her head to look out the car window instead of at her mother. They were sitting in the parking lot of the Seneca Hills Ice Arena on Friday evening.

Nikki, Danielle, and Haley were already inside the rink, finding good seats in the bleachers to watch Elyse practice for the benefit on Sunday night. The program included a pairs routine with Elyse and Blake, and then Elyse in a featured solo. Tori wanted to see the whole rehearsal. But she was stuck in the car, forced to listen to her mother lecture her for the hundredth time that week.

"I'm just trying to explain to you why it's so important for you to talk to Blake. Get him to agree to do a program for you," Mrs. Carsen said.

Tori tapped her foot impatiently. *Don't you think I know anything, Mother?* Tori wanted to say it, but she couldn't. Not right now. Somehow the words wouldn't come.

"Tori!"

"What!"

"Are you going to make an effort with Blake, or not?"

"It's probably too late anyway," Tori snapped. "I think Blake is going to start working with Nikki and Alex, or Danielle next."

Mrs. Carsen let out a loud sigh. "Are you sure?"

"No."

"Well, what makes you think that?"

"Nikki and Alex had to do their program for Blake yesterday, and then Dani told me that Blake was watching her practice this morning, and he talked to Mr. Weiler afterward."

"You see? That's what happens when you aren't aggressive enough," Mrs. Carsen said, throwing up her hands. "Now he's choosing someone else. If you had talked to Blake sooner—"

"I tried!" Tori said. "But I haven't run into him at the right time."

"Well, what about talking to Elyse? Have you asked her to help you? She seems to be very close to Blake, and—"

"Mother, Elyse is hardly ever around. And when she is, she doesn't want to be bothered with my problems. Or haven't you noticed?"

Mrs. Carsen was silent for a moment. "I suppose this means you haven't gotten her to teach you the Taylor layback yet either."

"No. I haven't," Tori admitted.

Mrs. Carsen closed her mouth tight and pursed her lips.

Please don't say anything else, Tori prayed. Just let me get out of this car.

"Okay, Tori," Mrs. Carsen said. "I can see that you're determined to handle these things your own way. But just remember. You'll have to handle the consequences, too, if the outcome of the Regional competition isn't what you expect."

Tori opened the car door, but then turned around and looked at her mother with a puzzled expression.

"I thought you were coming inside. To watch Elyse."

"I can't," Mrs. Carsen replied. "I have a business meeting with a client." She paused, then let her face relax a little. "Besides," she admitted, "I'm getting sort of sick of Elyse Taylor."

"Me too," Tori said. She and her mother exchanged smiles, and the tension between them evaporated a little.

"See you later, Mom," Tori called. She climbed out, then pushed the car door shut and hurried inside the rink. Tori didn't want to miss a thing. Maybe she'd try extra hard to talk to Blake tonight. It sure would make her mother happy.

Inside the figure-skating rink Tori paused. To-

night the usually quiet rink was buzzing with excitement. On the ice Elyse was warming up for her
pairs program, while people from the town, including a horde of TV and newspaper reporters, filled
the bleachers.

Suddenly Tori spotted Blake near the boards getting ready to step onto the ice. He removed his skate
guards, then pulled his navy-and-white ski sweater
over his head. He tossed it onto one of the seats in
the bleachers near where Nikki and Danielle were
sitting with Haley and Patrick.

Tori quickly joined her friends.

"Hey," Haley called to her. "I don't think Elyse is
letting the fact that she missed our lunch date affect
her performance too much. She's looking great in
warm-ups."

Tori grimaced, but didn't say anything. Who cares
about her performance? she thought. The only thing
Tori was worrying about now was getting Blake to
work with her next.

Suddenly her eye fell upon Blake's sweater lying
on the bleachers. On impulse she picked it up and
pulled it over her head. It was so big, it fit easily
over the thin white turtleneck top she wore.

Good thing I changed into navy stretch pants, Tori
thought.

The navy-blue-and-white ski sweater was huge on
her, which made it look just right with her skintight
pants. And it perfectly matched her navy-blue ankle-
high boots, too.

"Nice sweater." Danielle cocked an eyebrow as she noticed Tori rolling up the enormous sleeves. "Planning to keep it?"

Tori was about to tell her friend she was just borrowing it, when a fabulous idea occurred to her.

Maybe I *won't* give it back, she thought. I'll keep the sweater until Blake decides to work with me.

Tori was so pleased with herself, she almost laughed out loud.

She knew it was a silly idea, but it just might work. At the very least, wearing the sweater would provide her with an excuse to talk to Blake for a few minutes.

Tori crossed her arms and hugged the sweater to her as the skaters finished warming up. Soon the strains of their program music, the theme from the movie *Love Story*, filled the hushed arena. The lights were dimmed even lower, and on the ice Elyse and Blake joined hands as they began their romantic duet.

From the very beginning the crowd was mesmerized. Even Tori, who'd been fuming at Elyse all day, was awed once again by the skater's elegance. Elyse and Blake weren't pairs partners, but they seemed to flow into each other with the kind of smoothness and gracefulness that only practiced pairs could achieve.

Next to Tori, Nikki seemed to be thinking the same thing. "Now I know what Alex and I are working toward," she murmured.

When the rehearsal ended, Tori jumped to her feet, though not to applaud along with everyone else in the crowded arena. Instead she rushed down to the edge of the rink, calling over her shoulder to her friends, "Be right back. I have to talk to Blake."

Her timing was perfect. She reached the barrier just as Blake was exiting the ice.

"Hey—that looks better on you than it does on me," he said with a lopsided grin when he saw Tori and noticed the sweater.

She smiled and cocked her head. "I'm not giving it back."

"Never?" Blake asked, playing along.

"Never," Tori said. "Or at least not until you promise to work with me next. Right after you're done working with Haley and Patrick."

The smile flew off Blake's face. "Keep the sweater," he mumbled. Then he reached down, put on his skate guards, and walked off.

Tori's heart sank. Oh no, she thought. Now I've done it. She wasn't certain, but it sure seemed as if Blake was angry that she'd asked him to work with her.

Danielle and Nikki appeared at her side.

"What did Blake say about the sweater?" Danielle asked eagerly. "Did he notice you were wearing it?"

"He noticed," Tori mumbled.

"So what'd he say?" Danielle pressed her.

"He said I could keep it," Tori answered truthfully.

"Really?" Danielle sounded jealous.

"Yes," Tori said, trying to recover her composure. "And since it goes so well with these pants, I think I'll wear it to school on Monday!"

Her friends laughed, and Tori faked a giggle as if she'd amused herself, too. But inside she felt miserable. Blake would probably never talk to her again, let alone choreograph her program.

9

Early Saturday morning the phone in Tori's room rang, waking her up. "Great," she mumbled. "One of my only days to sleep late and I can't even catch a few extra Zs."

She reached for the black phone that sat on her nightstand. "Hello?"

"Tori, I need you. Help!"

It was Haley on the other end.

"What's up?" Tori asked.

"I'm going crazy," Haley said. "I'm at the rink, and Patrick and I have been working like crazy on our new program, and Blake is really pushing us. We've been here since six A.M.—and it's *Saturday!*" Haley said it all in one breath. "It feels like I haven't done anything but skate and think about my career for months and months."

"Me too," Tori agreed with a sigh. The memory of Blake's face when she'd asked him about working with her flooded back into her mind. How could she have acted so stupid and immature? This morning she wanted nothing to do with Silver Blades, or Blake Michaels, or Elyse Taylor.

"So? Do you want to go to the mall or what?" Haley asked.

"We were just there yesterday," Tori reminded her. "For lunch. Remember?"

"I don't care," Haley said. "I need another break. Let's go."

"Okay," Tori decided. "But I'd better get some practice time in this afternoon."

"That's cool," Haley said. "Just get *me* out of here for a while!"

By early afternoon Tori and Haley were burned out on shopping. They had already done everything—hung out at the music store listening to the newest CDs and tapes on headphones, spent an hour trying on clothes in a department store, and then had lunch. They even ran into and talked to some cute eighth-grade guys from school.

It had been a relief to get away from the Ice Arena for a while, but now Tori knew that she needed to get back there and practice.

"Let's go," she told Haley. "I'll call my mom and get a ride."

When the girls got to the rink thirty minutes later, Tori anxiously scanned the lobby for signs of Blake. She was embarrassed to face him, but there was a part of her that wanted to get it over with. Maybe if she approached him differently this time . . . or said she was sorry.

"Tori!"

Tori recognized the sharp voice instantly. It was the Sarge.

"Tori, I want to talk to you for a moment," Kathy barked. *"Privately."*

The coach turned on her heel and marched down the hall to her office.

Tori's stomach was in knots. She had a feeling she knew what this was about.

In Kathy's office Tori dropped into one of the chairs.

Kathy sat down behind the desk and faced her with a serious expression. "So when are you planning to return my book?" Kathy asked.

Tori swallowed. "Uh, I'm not quite done with it," she fumbled. "May I keep it for another few days?"

"No." Kathy shook her head. "I lent it to you almost a week ago, and now I'd like it back."

"Well," Tori stalled, desperately trying to think of something. "The thing is, I, um, left it in my mother's office. I don't think I can get it back until Monday."

"That's not true, Tori, and you know it," Kathy said evenly. "And I'm deeply disturbed that you've decided to lie to me instead of telling the truth."

Tori felt the color drain from her face. "I'm *not* lying!" she managed to protest.

Kathy stared at her. "Until you're ready to tell me the truth, I don't want to talk to you about it."

Tori stood up, her knees shaking. She tried to keep her expression calm.

"I'm sorry you don't believe me," she said with an indignant sniff. "I guess you've made your mind up, and there's nothing I can do."

Kathy shook her head. "All I can tell you, Tori, is this. Right now what's important to you is your skating career. But one day you're going to wish that you'd spent more time developing a sense of responsibility and honesty about things that have nothing to do with skating."

Tori felt tears welling up in her eyes. Fortunately Kathy didn't see them, because she had already turned away to some papers on her desk.

Brushing the tears away quickly, Tori swallowed hard.

What nerve, Tori thought. She's accusing me of lying! Even though it was true, Kathy couldn't possibly know that. She didn't have any proof.

Besides, Tori thought, it's not my fault that Elyse took the book. She whirled around and marched into the hallway.

Haley was waiting for her outside Kathy's office.

"What was that all about?" Haley asked.

"Oh, nothing. I just think Kathy's the meanest coach, that's all," Tori said angrily.

A look of surprise crossed Haley's face, and Tori knew why. Haley had never heard Tori talk that way about Kathy before.

Haley shrugged. "Okay. I think I'll go get changed," she said. "Coming?"

Tori shook her head. "I need to talk to Elyse," she said grimly.

While Haley headed for the locker room, Tori stomped toward the rink. Outside the doors she bumped into Patrick, Haley's skating partner.

"Hey, Tori," he called. "Seen Haley?"

"She's in the locker room," Tori told him. "She'll be out in a minute." She smiled at him.

Tall and good-looking, with warm brown eyes and red hair, Patrick was a great match for Haley. Except for their height, they almost looked like twin brother and sister. And lately Patrick had even started wearing wilder clothes and an earring to match his partner's style. Today he had on a pair of baggy purple jeans and a white T-shirt.

"We can't get on the ice for ten more minutes. Not until Elyse finishes rehearsing," Patrick said, jerking his thumb in the direction of the figure-skating rink.

Without thinking, Tori rolled her eyes.

Patrick's eyes twinkled. "Getting sick of the ice princess?"

Tori shook her head. "No," she told him quickly. "I'm just eager to start practice. See you later."

She entered the rink and immediately spotted Blake at one end of the ice. He was watching Elyse rehearse her long program.

Tori sat down in the seats to watch. She wanted to talk to Elyse about Kathy's book, but obviously it would have to wait. A few minutes later Haley and Patrick joined her.

"She's incredible," Patrick remarked when Elyse landed a beautiful triple-double combination.

Tori had to agree. Elyse's program was filled with good, strong jumps and an elegant line. Tori had never seen a more graceful or intense skater.

Finally the taped music stopped on a high note, just as Elyse completed a high-speed scratch spin in the middle of the ice.

"Brava!" Blake called, clapping.

Immediately Tori jumped up and hurried down to meet Elyse as she came off the ice. But Elyse ignored her and turned to Blake. She smoothed her auburn hair, giving him a huge smile.

"That felt great," she said. "Do you think I'm still in top form? Like at the Olympics?"

Blake nodded. "Absolutely."

"Elyse," Tori began. "I need to talk to you about the book I—"

Elyse cut her off right away. "Tori," she said sharply, "I'm rehearsing. You'll have to talk to me later."

Tori simmered. What am I supposed to do? she thought angrily. Wait around all day until she's ready to listen to me?

Then Elyse took Blake's arm and started leading him toward the locker rooms.

Tori blew out her breath in frustration. She was so sick of Elyse Talyor. No matter what, Elyse always seemed to get her way.

Tori stood at the side of the rink, watching as Haley and Patrick took to the ice to practice their new program.

Haley popped their music cassette into the tape machine. Then she and Patrick warmed up a bit before striking their opening pose in the middle of the ice.

Wow, Tori thought as she watched their first move. It was a star-lift, timed perfectly with the music. As the chords reached a crescendo, Patrick held Haley over his head, his hand on her thigh, while he spun in big circles. Then she came down and skated in large circles around him while he moved constantly forward, changing steps. It looked as if she were chasing him, and when she finally caught up to him, she draped herself over his leg while he spun in circles as if he were trying to get away.

The rest of the program was spectacular, too. Together Haley and Patrick completed one difficult jump after another and ended with side-by-side flying camels. At the very end Patrick took one extra revolution and grabbed Haley's hand, instantly pulling her into a difficult move called the death spiral.

"That's incredible," Tori said under her breath.

That's what Blake Michaels can do, she realized with excitement. Now she had to try to talk to him again. Even if he was still angry at her, she could talk him into working with her—she just knew she could.

Tori hurried into the women's locker room.

Elyse was in there getting changed. "I don't have time for a conversation now," she said quickly when she saw Tori's reflection in the mirror. "I'm doing a TV interview in five minutes."

"That's fine," Tori snapped. I didn't come in here to talk to you anyway, she thought.

Tori opened her skating bag and looked inside. Yup. Blake's sweater was still there.

This is my chance, she thought. It was now or never. Her hands trembling, Tori pulled Blake's sweater on over her clothes and rushed out to the parking lot.

A moment later she found Blake's black Honda Del Sol.

You shouldn't be doing this, she told herself, her heart pounding in double time. She walked over to his car and tried a door handle.

Yes! It was unlocked.

Tori slid into the black leather passenger's seat and settled in to wait for him. She let out a long, nervous breath.

At least now you can't ignore me, Blake Michaels.

10

As Tori sat waiting for Blake, she glanced around his car. What did he have in here, anyway? Maybe learning more about him would help her to figure out what to say to him and how to win him over. Stuffed behind the driver's seat were two T-shirts and a black baseball cap. A pile of skating magazines lay on the floor beside a candy-bar wrapper and a towel.

Then Tori flipped through his cassette collection. It was weird how many different kinds of music Blake liked. Classical. Rock. Pop. Jazz.

Maybe it's because he's a choreographer now, she thought. He has to listen to everything.

Next, with a pang of guilt, she opened the glove compartment and found some papers and a letter

addressed in big, scrawly handwriting. Tori had
seen Elyse sign so many autographs, she immediately recognized the handwriting.

Tori held it in her hands. She was dying to read
it. But Kathy's words about personal responsibility
and honesty floated back into her head. Reluctantly
she put the letter back in the glove compartment.
Reading someone else's mail was wrong, and Tori
knew it.

Suddenly the driver's side door jerked open and
Tori looked up, startled.

"What are you doing in here?" Blake sounded
stern.

"Hi," she said nervously. "Surprise!"

Blake shook his head disapprovingly. "It sure is
a surprise," he said, climbing into the driver's seat.
"What's up?"

"I just wanted to return your sweater," Tori said.

"Uh, right," Blake said sarcastically. "Only it looks
to me like we've got a problem here. You're still
wearing it."

"Yeah." Tori giggled.

"Look, Tori," Blake began. "I'm in a hurry right
now. I've got to go."

Blake turned the key in the ignition. He obviously
wanted her to get out of the car.

"Wait!" Tori said urgently. "I need to talk to you
about something."

"Let me guess," Blake said. "You want me to

work with you next, after I'm done with Haley and Patrick."

Tori looked into his blue eyes and nodded.

Blake paused.

"Look, Tori," he said. "I've already decided who I want to work with next. And believe it or not, you're it."

Tori's heart jumped into her throat. Blake was planning to work with her next?

"Really?" she asked.

He nodded. "I've got to be honest with you. I am not impressed by cute tricks to get my attention. I've chosen you because you have talent. It's your skating that counts—not stealing my sweater." He paused as she looked away, her face flaming.

"I've seen a lot of skaters—one in particular—act insincere and use people to get what they want for their careers. Do yourself a favor and concentrate on improving your skating, not on trying to impress the world."

Tori nodded, barely trusting herself to speak. Then she pulled Blake's sweater off over her head and tossed it onto the backseat.

"Thank you," she whispered softly, then climbed out of the car.

As she headed back toward the rink, a lump gathered in her throat. Soon she would have a chance to work with Blake, but she knew she had a lot to think about in the meantime.

Today two people had warned her about her behavior: first Kathy Bart, and now Blake. And deep down Tori knew that she deserved the harsh words and warnings in both instances. She'd seen firsthand how Elyse treated people and she didn't want to wind up acting like that. Tori didn't ever want to be an ice princess—even if she did make it all the way to the Olympics.

Tori swallowed hard, also remembering how competitive she'd been around her friends. More than once she'd lied to them, not only to make them think Elyse was treating her well, but also to get Blake to choose her first. In some ways she'd acted as bad as Elyse—and maybe even worse.

As Kathy had said, there were some things that were worth more than a gold medal—such as her friendship with Dani, Nikki, and Haley.

When Tori entered the rink a few minutes later, Haley shouted to her from across the lobby.

"Tori. Where've you been?"

"Talking to Blake," Tori said as her friend rushed over. "Guess what. He's going to work with me as soon as he's done with you guys."

"Cool!" Haley said. She peered at Tori closely. "So why aren't you jumping up and down and shrieking? Did he tell you how hard he works you?"

Tori shrugged. "I'm willing to work hard—that's not it. It's just . . ." Her words trailed off as she struggled to explain. But Haley barely noticed her hesitation.

"Right." Haley shook her head. "About a month from now just remember you said that."

"Why? What happens in a month?" Tori asked.

"I figure that's when you'll be calling *me* and begging *me* to take you to the mall on Saturdays!" Haley said with a laugh.

Tori wrapped an arm around her friend. "I hope you're right," she said.

The stars were sparkling bright in the dark sky by the time Tori returned home from the rink. Tori loved this kind of night, when it was cold and crystal clear outside.

After Haley's parents dropped her off, she lingered in the driveway for a minute staring at the sky. Usually I make a wish on the brightest star, Tori thought. But now that Blake had made his decision, Tori didn't know what to wish for. Somehow tonight she felt as though she had everything she needed.

Except for one thing. The book. She had to get Kathy's book back.

But that isn't something to wish for, Tori thought. I have to make that happen all by myself.

Elyse's car stood in the driveway. Tori took a deep breath and headed into the house.

The skater was sprawled on the sofa in the living

room with her feet up on the coffee table, drinking soda and reading a magazine.

"Oh, hi! What a day! Am I glad to have someone to talk to!" Elyse patted a sofa cushion near her, indicating that Tori should sit down.

This is typical, Tori thought. She always turns sweet when she wants something. Or when she wants to get away with something. I wonder what it is.

"Wait till you see these pictures!" Elyse said in a giddy tone. She held up the skating magazine she was reading. "It's the Juvenile National champions. A bunch of scrawny baby skaters with gangly arms and legs. They look like little spiders to me. Don't you think so?"

"Listen, Elyse," Tori said, ignoring her comments. "I'm really tired and I'm going to go up and take a hot bath. But first I need to get that book back from you."

"What book?" Elyse asked.

Tori was so shocked, for a minute she couldn't speak. How could Elyse even ask that question? "The Margo DeForest autobiography," Tori reminded her. "The one you took with you when you went to meet Blake for dinner a few nights ago."

"Oh, I don't know where I put it," Elyse said. "And I'm much too tired to go look for it now. Can't it wait?"

"No. Just tell me where to look," Tori said firmly. "*I'll* find it."

Elyse slapped the magazine down onto the coffee table and let out a groan.

"Look," she finally said, "I don't know why you're making such a big deal about this book. But the truth is, I left it somewhere while I was out. I have no idea where. So you're just going to have to forgive me."

"You're kidding!" Tori cried. "I mean, I *told* you I didn't want you to take it anywhere!"

"It's not the end of the world," Elyse said. "It's just a book."

Tori's face burned. Her eyes started to fill with tears, but she fought them back.

"Look, I'll make it up to you," Elyse said. "Maybe tomorrow morning we can go to the rink early and I'll teach you the Taylor layback."

"Yeah, right," Tori said. "I really believe that. You've been promising to do things for me all week, and you never do them. You never show up. You never keep your promises."

"Well, what do you want? Money?" Elyse said nastily. "How much is the stupid book worth?" She stood up as if she were going up to her room right then to get the money. "I'll be happy to pay you for it."

"I don't want money," Tori said, choking back angry tears. "I want the book. You had no right to take it! Can't you remember where you left it?"

Elyse threw her hands up in the air. "This is ridiculous!" she exploded. "I will not be grilled like

I'm some kind of criminal! It's just a book with a faded cover!"

With that Elyse stormed up the stairs and started slamming things around in her room. Twenty minutes later Elyse marched downstairs carrying her bags in both hands.

"Tell your mother I thank her *so much* for her hospitality," Elyse said in a nasty tone. "I'm going to the Circle Tower Hotel—where I should have gone in the first place! If anyone calls, they can reach me there."

"I doubt if anyone will call," Tori replied. "You don't seem to have too many friends."

Elyse glared at Tori for a moment. "*You* don't know anything about what it takes to be an Olympic champion," Elyse said, spitting the words out. "And you *never* will. And by the way, Tori. I know why you've been hanging around Blake all week. You're hoping that he'll do a program for you next. Well, you can kiss that idea good-bye."

"That's what you think," Tori retorted. "Blake just told me—he's picked me to work with next."

"Ha!" Elyse said. "Well, after I talk to him, he'll never work with you as long as he lives!"

Tori watched her leave through the front door. As usual it was a dramatic exit; Elyse held her head as stiffly and proudly as a queen as she swept through the doorway, her beautiful leather luggage in hand.

Maybe Elyse would talk to Blake about Tori and

try to ruin her career. But somehow it didn't even matter anymore. Tori no longer felt respect or admiration for Elyse Taylor. Instead, all she felt was a strong dose of pity.

11

"**S**hhh! She's still asleep! Don't wake her," someone whispered near Tori's head.

"She's sleeping with her mouth open," another voice said. Then Tori heard giggles.

Tori stirred under the covers. She was dreaming that there were people in her room whispering about her and watching her sleep.

"Put the tray on the floor by her bed," someone said. It sounded like Dani. "So she'll see it when she first wakes up."

Tori pulled her white comforter up closer to her ears and snuggled down under it to keep warm.

"She's never going to wake up," a voice complained. "I told you this was a flaky idea."

That's Haley, Tori realized, opening one eye just

enough to look around. Haley, Danielle, and Nikki were all standing there staring at her.

"Hey," Tori said, sitting up in bed all of a sudden. "What are you guys doing here?"

Tori's friends laughed and crowded around. Haley plopped down on the floor, while Nikki and Danielle sat on the covers at the end of her bed.

"We heard about everything," Nikki said quickly. "So we came over to cheer you up."

"Yeah—but who knew you were going to sleep till *noon*?" Haley complained jokingly.

Tori rubbed her eyes. What day was it? Oh, yeah— Sunday. Yesterday seemed like years ago. Then Tori remembered what had happened. Elyse had left last night in a huff.

"You heard *what*?" Tori asked.

"Everything," Dani said. "Haley told us about your fight with Kathy. And how Kathy yelled at you."

"I couldn't help overhearing some of it in the hall," Haley said apologetically. "I didn't want to tell you yesterday. You seemed so upset."

"And then when we called here last night, your mom told us about Elyse," Nikki said. "We figured you were really upset."

"And when we called this morning, she said you were *still* sleeping!" Haley added. "Are you okay?"

Tori nodded. "But my stomach is growling. I'm starved."

"That's why we brought you breakfast in bed!" Danielle announced happily. "Including homemade coffee cake baked by my grandmother!"

Tori looked down at the tray on the floor. Orange juice. Coffee cake. Cereal. Fruit. Cottage cheese. And even a small vase with a flower in it.

"I don't believe this," Tori said. "You guys are so nice!"

"Unlike *someone* we know," Haley said. "Someone who recently won a gold medal."

"Yeah," Tori said. She looked right at Haley. "I have to admit you were right about her. She's a complete fake, and selfish and nasty, too."

"So why did she leave?" Nikki asked.

Tori sat all the way up in bed and propped up pillows behind her back. She eyed the tray of food hungrily. "Let me eat something and then I'll tell you everything."

"Okay," Nikki said. "But let's call Jill and put her on the speaker phone. You know she'll want to hear every detail."

Tori winced. "Yeah," she said. "Jill was right about Elyse from the beginning. She tried to tell me, but I wouldn't listen."

Tori took a big bite of coffee cake and then a gulp of orange juice. Meanwhile Nikki called Jill.

"Hi!" Jill said, talking on the phone in her dorm hallway. "Hey, Tori. Are you there?"

"Ymmessn," Tori said, her mouth full of food.

Everyone laughed.

"Tori, I wanted to tell you that I've heard about what's been going on from Nikki and Dani—and I'm sorry you had to go through all of this. I mean,

I'm sorry you had to learn about Elyse the hard way."

"Thanks, Jill," Tori said gratefully. "I should have listened to you."

Tori ate her cereal while Nikki, Dani, and Haley gossiped with Jill. Then, when she had finished eating the last of the coffee cake, she filled her friends in on all the details about Elyse, Kathy's book, and Elyse's stormy departure the night before.

"And I lied about these earrings, too," Tori confessed. "Elyse didn't give them to me. My mom did."

"Oh." Her friends sounded as if they felt sorry for her.

"But that's really great about Blake," Nikki said. "I mean, that he's going to work with you next."

"Definitely," Danielle agreed. "We're all really happy for you, Tori. You deserve it."

Tori hesitated. She'd told her friends about Blake's working with her next, but she hadn't told them all the details about what he'd said to her. She was still thinking about that. "I'm glad he picked me," she admitted. "Now I'm just worried Elyse will talk him out of it."

"I doubt it," Haley said. "I've been around Blake a lot. He doesn't seem like that kind of person to me."

"I hope not," Tori said. "I feel like such a jerk, though. I think I made a fool of myself."

"At least you didn't try to bribe him with a chocolate cake." Danielle giggled.

Tori grinned. "Yeah, Dani. That was a *huge* cake."

"But what about Kathy's book? You're never going to get it back, are you?" Haley asked.

Tori shook her head. "I guess not."

"Yikes," Jill said on the phone. "The Sarge is going to kill you."

"I know," Tori replied. "Do you think she'll believe it if I tell her my mom ate her skating book?"

Everyone laughed, but Nikki shook her head. "No way," she said. "You've got to tell her the truth. Tell her that Elyse borrowed it and lost it, that's all."

Tori thought about that. She knew Nikki was right, but it seemed too hard. Could she really face up to Kathy that way, and admit she lied?

"I'll try," Tori said. "But I don't know. The main thing is that I'm really sorry I lied to you guys and tried to pretend Elyse was so sweet. I guess I just wanted it to be true."

"Yeah. But that's *not* the main thing," Haley said.

"What is?"

"The main thing is that after tonight Seneca Hills will be rid of Elyse Taylor—for good!" Haley declared.

"Yes!" Tori said with a cheer, and Nikki, Danielle, Haley, and Jill joined in.

All the Silver Blades skaters arrived at the rink by four o'clock Sunday afternoon. As members of the club, the skaters and their parents had the privilege of coming early so they could watch Elyse and Blake warm up for the benefit program that night.

Tori wanted to watch, too, but first she had to wait for Kathy. She knew if she didn't talk to Kathy soon, she'd lose her nerve.

Pacing in the lobby, she watched each person enter through the arena's front doors.

"Hey—aren't you coming inside?"

The voice behind Tori startled her. She whirled around and saw Blake standing there in his costume—a simple black unitard and a white silk shirt with huge flowing sleeves.

"Uh, yeah," Tori said nervously. "I'm just waiting for someone. Aren't you and Elyse warming up?"

"Her Majesty sent me out here to get her a diet soda," Blake said with a roll of his eyes. He looked down at the can of soda in his hands. "I'm tempted to shake it up," he said devilishly. "But I guess I'd better not."

Tori laughed. "She's pretty amazing."

"Yeah," Blake said. "I hear you two had a big blowup last night. Sorry. I shouldn't have stuck you with her this week."

"Oh, that's okay," Tori said quickly. She opened her mouth to ask Blake if Elyse had said anything bad about her, but stopped herself.

"Don't worry," Blake said, reading Tori's mind. "She tried to tell me what a lousy skater you are and that I shouldn't work with you—ever. But I've got eyes. I know good skating when I see it."

Tori breathed a sigh of relief.

"I know an ice princess when I see one, too," Blake said lightly. "Remember what I told you yesterday. Don't ever let that happen to you, Tori."

With that he gave Tori a wink and headed back toward the ice.

Just then Tori heard Kathy's voice in the crowded lobby. Tori turned and hurried to catch up with her.

"What is it, Tori?" Kathy asked when she noticed Tori following her into her office.

Tori looked at the floor, then up at Kathy again. "I have something I need to tell you. About the book you lent to me."

Kathy waited patiently.

"I'm really sorry," Tori started, "but Elyse Taylor borrowed your book from me, and then she lost it. I feel horrible about it. I know I shouldn't have let her take it, but I couldn't stop her."

Tori looked away quickly, afraid to meet Kathy's eyes. Kathy kept silent for a moment. Then she said softly, "I'm glad you finally told me the truth, Tori. That's the most important thing."

"I'm sorry I lied about it before," Tori said.

"Well . . ." Kathy paused as if she wasn't sure whether she should say what she was thinking. "As your skating career progresses, Tori, you're going to meet a lot of famous skaters. And I'm afraid you're going to find out that they're not all champions at heart."

Champions at heart. That was a familiar phrase. Tori had the funny feeling she'd just read it somewhere.

"Elyse is a good example," Kathy continued. "Most people in the top levels of skating know that Elyse puts on a good-girl act for the media. But she's really not very nice in person. So I'm not surprised that she took advantage of you that way."

"I shouldn't have fallen for it," Tori said.

"You can't expect yourself to be perfect, Tori. Or to know everything. And besides. There's something else you need to realize, too. Elyse is still very young—and she's under a lot of pressure. It's not easy dealing with all the fame and the attention that go with winning a gold medal. I think you probably ran into Elyse Taylor at the worst possible time," Kathy concluded.

Maybe, Tori thought. But that was no excuse for the way Elyse acted.

Kathy moved some papers from her desktop to a drawer and hung her winter coat on a rack in the corner. Then she turned to Tori and rubbed her hands together. "But no matter what I think of Elyse personally, I don't want to miss seeing her skate. Do you?"

"No," Tori said. "But can I ask you one question?" Kathy nodded. "How did you know I was lying about your book?"

A small smile crossed Kathy's face as she reached over toward her bookshelf. Tori followed her gaze, and her mouth fell open when she saw what Kathy reached for. It was the faded red copy of *My Story* by Margo DeForest!

"You found it? But when? How?" Tori was astonished.

"The manager of the Circle Tower Hotel called me a few days ago," Kathy explained. "He said that someone had left a book on a table in the lobby, and when he read the inscription inside, he recognized my name. I picked the book up that day."

"Thank goodness," Tori said, relieved. "I'm so glad you got it back!"

For an instant Tori stared at the book longingly. She still hadn't finished reading it, and right now—after spending a week with Elyse—Margo DeForest's inspiring story appealed to her even more.

Now, *there* was a skater who really was a champion at heart, Tori thought.

And then suddenly Tori remembered. That's where she had read it—the inscription in the front of Kathy's book: *To Kathy Bart, a fine young skater with the heart of a champion.*

"I'm really sorry," Tori told Kathy again.

"That's okay," Kathy said, shooing Tori out the door. "Let's go."

Tori hurried back out to the ice rink and joined her friends in their seats. The program was about to start and everyone was excited.

"Hurry up!" Haley called, motioning to Tori. "You're missing the best scene!"

"What?"

Haley pointed to the television crew down near the ice. "They're interviewing Elyse, and she's practically drooling all over the interviewers. And a minute ago she was carrying around someone's baby from the audience. And skating with it!"

"I don't believe it," Tori said with disgust.

"She sure knows how to act when the camera is on," Nikki said.

"True," Tori said. "But what's she wearing in her hair? That's the ugliest feather headdress I've ever seen!"

"Tori! You sound just like Elyse!" Dani scolded.

Tori blushed and then laughed. "You're right," she said. "I do get sort of catty sometimes. I'll have to work on that."

Suddenly Tori looked up at a small window high above the ice on the end wall of the skating rink. There, in the black sky, she saw a brilliant star.

I should make a wish, she thought. But instead she turned to her friends.

"Let's make a pact," she said solemnly. "Let's promise each other that we'll never turn into ice princesses—no matter how famous we become."

"It's a deal," Nikki said quickly.

"Definitely," Danielle agreed.

"No sweat. I promise," Haley said.

"Me too," Tori said. "And you have to promise one

more thing. Promise that we'll always stick together and watch out for each other. I mean, if you see me slipping—starting to act like Elyse—"

"Don't worry," Haley said, putting her arm around Tori. "If you start acting like a princess, we'll just break into your house and take all your tiaras away!"

Tori giggled happily along with her friends. "Will you promise to steal my feather headdresses, too?"

"Absolutely," Haley promised.

Then the four of them turned back to the ice to watch Elyse's final performance in Seneca Hills.

#4: Going for the Gold

It's a dream come true! Jill's going to the famous figure-skating center in Colorado. But the training is *much* tougher than Jill ever expected, and Kevin, a really cute skater at the school, has a plan that's sure to get her into *big* trouble. Could this be the end of Jill's skating career?

#5: The Perfect Pair

Nikki Simon and Alex Beekman are the perfect pair on the ice. But off the ice there's big trouble. Suddenly Alex is sending Nikki gifts and asking her out on dates. Nikki wants to be Alex's partner in pairs but not his girlfriend. Will she lose Alex when she tells him? Can Nikki's friends in Silver Blades find a way to save her friendship with Alex *and* her skating career?

#6: Skating Camp

Summer's here and Jill Wong can't wait to join her best friends from Silver Blades at skating camp. It's going to be just like old times. But things have changed since Jill left Silver Blades to train at a famous ice academy. Tori and Danielle are spending all their time with another skater, Haley Arthur, and Nikki has a big secret that she won't share with anyone. Has Jill lost her best friends forever?